Mama B: A Time to Plant
a novella

By Michelle Stimpson

Published by Read for Joy, an Imprint of MLStimpson Enterprises
MichelleStimpson.com

Dedication

For my sisters in the Lord who help me grow up.
I appreciate you!

Acknowledgments

Thank you, Abba Father, for yet another book. This is amazing to me! But I suppose I shouldn't be surprised what You do in me since You are infinite. I'm glad to be along for the ride.

Thank you to all my readers and avid Mama B fans. Sorry to keep you waiting so long! I missed Mama B, too! I hope you'll enjoy her again and share with your friends.

Thanks to my critique group for helping me keep Mama B's voice consistent: Janice, Jan, Dana, Jackie, Ann, Lyndie, Pattie, and Vickie. You all help me tremendously and I appreciate you. Thanks to my informal book cover committee: April Barker, Tia McCollors, and CaSandra McLaughlin, who also helped flesh out the plot along with Vanessa Miller. Thanks Karen McCollum-Rodgers, the editor. I hope you're enjoying the Mama B ride, too.

Thanks to Tamara Davis and Eugenia Washington for reading the third draft and giving critical feedback. Love you ladies!

And special thanks to Officer Lorena Villalva and Porfirio Limones with Dallas County Corrections Department for the insight on matters pertaining to jail. And right here I have to give praise again that I had to go ask somebody about jail because I surely don't know about them first-hand, thank God!

Finally, thanks to my family. At the end of the day, you all are the people I wish to come home to. Thanks for always being there.

Chapter 1

Pastor Phillips and Ophelia fancied themselves taking off on a second honeymoon to celebrate their second anniversary. I suppose at our ages—the 70s and 80s—we got to celebrate every milestone 'cause we ain't got too many more rocks left on the path.

Sunday afternoon, I ended up driving Pastor, Ophelia, and Frank to the airport in Dallas. Frank was headed to a doctor's convention in Chicago for the week. Pastor and Ophelia were off on a cruise to Mexico and Jamaica, partly courtesy of the Pastor's Appreciation Committee.

Nowadays pastors come and go. Some get burned out, some fall off the wagon, and I imagine some just can't take living in the fishbowl. So after 40 years of service, Pastor Phillips deserved somethin' real, real nice.

The thing was, the best cruise rate for the anniversary trip happened to plop itself right in the middle of our fall revival time. Rev. Martin assured everyone that the revival would go on, even in Pastor's absence.

Pastor agreed, saying, "If Mount Zion can't operate without me for a week or so by now, we in a world of hurt already."

And so it was. Frank, Pastor, and Ophelia loaded up in the Range Rover so I could drop them off at DFW airport.

Frank nearly made me turn red when he patted my behind right there in front of Pastor as I shut the trunk door closed.

"Frank! Stop it!"

He still gets a kick out of teasin' me. "You know you're

gonna miss my pats. What are you going to do without me for a whole week?"

"Not sure, exactly. Might look into taking that sewing class at the library," I said.

Frank grimaced. "Come on now, Honey B. You're already involved in so much. Do you really need to add something else to your plate? Something else that will take time from us?"

Ophelia yelled all the way from the curb, "That's what I tell her all the time, Doc. She need to get somewhere and sit down. Relax."

I ignored my friend, who was always good for meddling. Turning my attention back to Frank, I said, "I'll wait until you get back. Maybe you and I can find another dancing class."

"Maybe so. But I don't need to go nowhere to have a good time with you," Frank said. "When I get home from work every day, I'm just fine sitting at the house enjoying your company, if you ask me."

"We'll see, honey." I reached behind his neck and he lowered his head so I could kiss him. "You have a great time at the convention."

"Will do."

I stepped up on the concrete to send off my dearest friends as well. Pastor prayed for everyone's traveling grace. We had one final group hug, then I had to get out of there before I overstayed my time in the drop-off lane.

It felt kind of funny to send off my two coverings—my husband and my pastor. But the Lord's always with me. He is the ultimate covering.

No sooner than I dropped them off, I set my mind on the

revival, which was to start that night. Plans for the week-long meeting had come together well. Rev. Martin made all the arrangements for a guest minister to preach every night. Angela, our church secretary, had created all the flyers and made sure the announcements got in the Peasner papers and such, plus the church Facebook page. My job was to help Angela make sure the guest minister was received with a bucket full of Mount Zion hospitality.

Now, usually I got to draw some kind of lines when we have a guest minister 'cause I don't want nobody to get the wrong idea about my kindness and think maybe I'm tryin' to land me another sweetheart. Couldn't be further from the truth—Frank Wilson is sweetheart enough for me.

But I wasn't worried about it this time because we had a woman coming. Evangelist and Prophetess Falanda Shaw-McPherson. Now that was a whole lotta names, if you ask me, but didn't nobody really ask me, seeing as my primary membership had been switched to Frank's church. I still don't know if it's right for me to serve at two churches, but I guessed I'd rather be caught serving too much than too little.

Anyhow, Angela was gone to pick up the guest minister from the airport. Me and some of the younger wives from our Titus 2 women's group, LaTonya and Janice, had straightened up the church and even got some fresh flowers for the pulpit to last for the week. Thought it would be nice since we had a woman coming and all. It wasn't the first time a woman had come to encourage us, but it wasn't common.

I knew some of the deacons couldn't have been too happy about her being there, but they musta got overruled.

After me and the girls made sure the building was tidy— every cushioned seat free of debris and every hymnal-holder

9

empty of trash—we went ahead and started praying.

We was just down on our knees calling out to the Lord, clapping our hands, taking turns bringing our praises and requests before Him—like the church mothers used to do in the old days.

I'm always happy to pray with the younger women. Their hearts be so full of despair sometimes, worrying about stuff that don't even need to be worried about, really. But then I remember how I was at their age—still tryin' to change my husband, frettin' over whether my kids was actually listening to the lessons and the warnings I gave them, wonderin' if we was gonna have enough money to cover this and that. And every single time, the answer was right there in the Bible—everything gonna work out fine because of His promises. I guess it just be harder to see that until you been here three or four generations, though.

That night we was focused on the revival, however. We asked for Him to send a Word through the minister, bound up the works of the enemy and prayed for people and families as they came to mind. We interceded for the nation and the governments of the world, too, since it's so much hatred spinning all around the earth. Oh my, did we ever have a time in prayer. And His presence pressed in on us something wonderful!

About thirty minutes later, our musician, Clive showed up along with that new girl, Kizzy, from the soprano section. She a big-boned girl with high yellow skin and sandy hair to match, and ever since she stood up as a visitor, Clive had been cuckoo for Kizzy. She led more songs than Dianna Ross did with the Supremes.

Anyhow, Clive claimed they needed to work on her part

before she led the song that night, but they wasn't fooling me. Them two had the hots for one another, and it was sure about time Clive settled himself down, so that worked for me.

Me and my praying buddies was glad to leave him and her in the sanctuary. We went to the fellowship hall to finish up our praying, only we didn't get down on our knees 'cause them floors way too hard.

The Lord understands.

Before we knew it, it was time for church to start. We had about ten faithful members there plus a few people from one of our sister churches, but Evangelist Prophetess Falanda Shaw-McPherson wasn't nowhere in sight.

Rev. Martin took the podium and opened up in prayer. Then he asked Henrietta to lead us in a few congregational hymns. Henrietta had that stroke a while back, so her speech was sometimes slurred and her memory was off, but somehow she still recalled those songs of old.

"My soul loves Jesus," she started off and we all joined in. "My soul loves Jesus, bless His name. He's a wonder in my soul…"

I could see Rev. Martin getting antsy in the pulpit. I sent a text message to Angela, since she the one who was supposed to pick up the guest.

Almost there, she replied.

I put two and two together and guessed either the flight was late or they must have hit some traffic coming the forty-or-so miles from DFW airport to Peasner, which ain't hard to do any day of the week.

Mother Ruby took over leading the songs as a few more people joined the audience. "Jesus I'll never forget, no never…"

We had to help her out on the different verses because she couldn't quite remember what she was promising to never forget. But she always chimed in on, "Jesus I'll never forget, no never!" and I'm sure He was quite pleased.

Well, it's only so many congregational songs you can sing before folk start getting restless. I saw Rev. Martin checking his phone. He signaled for Clive to bring the singing to a close.

Clive allowed Mother Ruby another round, then he slowed the organ's tempo to a close.

Next thing I knew, the church's swinging doors came flying open and here comes a woman with one of them—*I forget the name*—front hairline wigs flowing around her chubby face and down to her shoulders, wearing a black robe like she about to graduate from somewhere.

Then she started screaming to high heaven as she walked down the main aisle, "In the name of Jesus, I curse every lying tongue in this house! I come against every empty pocketbook in this building! I bind up every report of high blood pressure, diabetes, sickle cell anemia, down to the very bunions on your feet! Somebody shout Amen!"

"Amen," the congregation whispered as she stomped straight up to the pulpit.

Rev. Martin stepped to the side looking like he wasn't sure if he should help the lady up the steps or run for his life.

My first thoughts was: *She 'bout the rudest thing I ever seen! You don't walk into nobody's house and take over—especially not your Father's house!* For all she know, we could have been in the middle of a prayer or taking up an offering.

Angela came and sat right next to me on the second pew. She was carrying a cooler, I guessed full of water for the speaker.

We all sat dumbfounded for a moment as our guest slung that hair to the side and removed the microphone from its stand.

"Church, the devil tried to stop me from getting here tonight. My first flight was canceled. Had to get on another airline." She turned and faced Reverend Martin. "I'm not tryin' to be funny, man of God, but don't put another guest on that airline. Not unless it's first-class. Amen?"

I felt my neck snap back. *I remember a time when traveling evangelists paid their own way, sister.*

Reverend Martin nodded to her, as though he could make a decision about the budget. He know good and well Pastor Phillips got the last say-so.

She continued, "The heel on my shoe broke. My luggage didn't arrive with me. So I know beyond the shadow of a doubt that there is work to do here in little ole Peasner, Texas! I come this far by faith, and I won't turn around! Look at your neighbor and tell 'em 'God's gonna clean house this week'."

Angela turned to me, but I guess the look on my face told her I wasn't about to play sermon-says all week.

Instead, she whispered, "Hello, Mama B."

"Hey, sweetheart," I mumbled, trying to keep my composure.

We spent the next forty-five minutes being 'buked, scorned, and talked about sure as we're born. Not just us at Mount Zion—*every* church.

"The church ain't nothin' but a bunch of hypocrites!" the evangelist barked into the microphone, breathing all hard like she got asthma in the spirit. "Full of cheaters and beaters! A lot of women hip-switchin' and men twitchin'! Too many haters and cross-maters!"

Chile, I don't even know what that last one meant, but I knew real quick—with all that bad-talkin' people and yellin' with the speaker a few feet from my head, I was probably gonna be a pew-changin', ear-closin' member that week.

Chapter 2

That night, Evangelist Prophetess Apostle (she added one about halfway through the sermon) Falanda Shaw-McPherson had a prayer line. She said everybody in the building needed to come through the prayer line if we was going to have a successful revival.

"Church, revival starts with us. Not the government. Not the schools. Not the businesses. The *church*."

Well, that I could agree on. So I followed her directions. I got in the prayer line.

The first person who hopped in line was Henrietta.

The minister asked, "What do you want from the Lord, Mother?" She put the mic up to Henrietta's mouth.

"I been praying for the Lord to give me a new TV. My old one went out, and I been having to watch TV on somebody phone. My eyes can't take it no mo'."

Falanda chuckled slightly. "You know what? The Lord honors your faith. But I have to ask you before we ask Him for this. What do plan on watching once the Lord blesses you with this new television?"

Henrietta rubbed her chin for second. "My favorite one be Real Housewives of—"

"No ma'am!" the minister jerked the microphone back to her own lips. Her angry gaze swept across the entire congregation. "Saints of God! We have no business asking

God to bless us so that we can dishonor Him with what He has given us!"

She got a few amens but mostly blank stares 'cause I know for a fact most the folks in the house had something on they TV they wouldn't share on Facebook.

The minister swiveled her neck down so she could speak to Henrietta. "Mother, I am *not* going to pray for you to get a new TV. I'm gonna pray that you *don't* get a TV until you stop cheatin' the Lord out of His time! That's what you are—a cheater! The Bible says all cheaters, liars, whoremongers—oh my! I can't even think of all the names that just dropped in my spirit about you!"

Chile, Henrietta didn't have a chance to say nothin' in response 'cause the preacher near-bout slapped her palm on top of Henrietta's face and started praying. "Father! We need a miracle tonight! Free her from all this ratchetness!"

Now, seeing as I knew what Henrietta had been through, I couldn't disagree with the lady one hundred percent. *Henrietta* did need a new mind. I just know a new mind don't come about 'cause somebody calls you a whole bunch of nasty names.

Then the lady started pushing down on Henrietta's head. I could tell 'cause I was close enough to see the muscles flinch in her arm.

But Henrietta wasn't going down, though. She was standing straight and tall, fighting the push-down with her neck muscles, which had veins showing by then.

I tell you, it was a fight. Henrietta refused to be pushed back and fall down. Her jaw was set. Yet the lady, being much younger, was stronger.

"Loose here!" the evangelist yelled.

Clive was over there playing a fast song on the organ and everybody was still clapping like they didn't see this showdown taking place.

So instead of falling backward or bowing her head, Henrietta started squatting. I mean squattin' like she standin' over a gas station toilet!

Jesus!

I couldn't take it no more. I rushed up there to Henrietta's side and pulled her away from the evangelist. Sent her on over to the usher so Henrietta could take a seat before somebody got hurt.

What in heaven's name?

Of course, this left me next in line for prayer.

Now, I don't know what kind of expression she read on my face, but whatever it said, she knew better than to try to push me down for sure. When she asked me what I wanted from the Lord, I told her point-blank, "Wisdom to deal with folks' foolishness."

She blinked.

I didn't.

"Yes, ma'am." And she prayed like she had some sense.

When she took her hands off my head, for the first time I really looked at her. I got a sense that behind her loud, booming voice and all that demon-binding she professed, there was something else written in the premature lines on her face and the drooping under her eyes. *Is it fear? Depression? Anger? Insecurity, Lord?*

Well, whatever it was wasn't none of my business, because she wouldn't be staying with me, she would be staying at Peasner's Best Western hotel, which was just as nice as the bigger chain hotels.

A long time ago, when my first husband Albert—rest his soul—and I lived in the house behind the church, some of the traveling evangelists used to stay with us. My boys always hated visiting ministers because they had to give up their bedrooms for the preacher and their family for a few days.

These days, the church reserved the room for our guest at a hotel if they planned on staying in the city. Dependin' on where they was coming from, most of them just drove in for the evening services. No matter, we paid for all their transportation and reimbursed their meals, on top of an honorarium, which we believe is only right.

Most of the folks coming all the way out to Peasner wasn't no big-name preachers. We might have got them from recommendations by another church, or maybe somebody's nephew tryin' to start up his ministry. Mainly it was folks that ain't tryin' to get rich off the gospel, just preachin' because the Lord called them to share the good news of Christ, and there ain't no better reason to preach than that.

Whatever Evangelist Prophetess Apostle Falanda Shaw-McPherson's reason was for coming to Peasner, I gave it to the Lord. We are His people. The sheep of His pasture. Far as I can tell, He's pretty good at chastening His own and exposing those who aren't His in the first place.

But as soon as service dismissed, Angela pulled my arm and asked if I could take the guest minister to the hotel.

"My schedule got kind of thrown off with her flight delay. I still need to run a few errands before I go home tonight and I don't want to be out too late."

Shoot, I don't wanna be out late, either! Who you think I am—the Boogie man?

I swallowed my pride. Ain't like I had to get up and go to

work the next morning. "Sure will, honey."

"Thank you, Mama B. We really do miss you around Mount Zion, you know?"

"I'm still here, ain't I?"

"Yes, but since we have to share you with Dr. Frank and his church, it's not the same."

I hugged her. "Well, feel free to call me anytime, Angela. I'm always here."

Her eyes moistened. "I will."

Lord, now this girl got a problem, too?

I knew right then the first thing I needed to do was get home and get alone with the Lord. Angela was a steady, faithful member of Mount Zion. If she started cracking up, wasn't no telling what the enemy could do at the church.

Maybe the evangelist was right about Mount Zion. And since I'd been going back and forth between churches, just like Angela said, maybe I had missed something.

Why hasn't Ophelia said anything?

Our guest barged into Angela's and my personal space. "Sister, I'm ready to depart this place."

The scowl the prophetess wore on her face made me wonder if my nose was working properly because she looked like she smelled something foul in the air.

"Hello. My name is Mama B," I introduced myself.

"God bless you, woman of God," she over-enunciated.

Then she turned back to Angela, her leaned-in posture demanding a response.

Angela shuffled a step backward even as she gave the minister the water cooler. "Mama B will be taking you to your hotel."

The prophetess swung her hair around. "Oh. Fine with me.

Mama B, are you ready?"

"Ready if you are."

She took off for the door, not even saying goodbye to Angela or greeting the people who had come out to support her. That's not how we do it in the country. Half the fun of a revival is meeting and fellowshipping with your brothers and sisters in Christ.

"I'll get her bags out of my car and bring them to yours," Angela said before she followed Miss Evangelist.

"I'm in Frank's truck," I yelled to her.

"Yes, ma'am," Angela threw over her shoulder.

Quickly, I made my way over to Rev. Martin, who was turning off the electricity to the microphone. The church folk were nearing the exit doors.

"Uh, excuse me."

He joined me on the ground level.

"Where did y'all get her from?"

He couldn't even look at me. "Somebody the Dukes knew."

Lord, I should have known. Well, let me back up. I like the Dukes. *Now.* But I didn't at first. The preacher and his wife came to minister at Mount Zion back when Pastor Phillips was taking care of his first wife, our beloved Geneva, in her last days, before she died of cancer. I had to put a stop to the Dukes' shenanigans, trying to make God out like He's a scratch-off lotto ticket.

Once we came to an understanding in love, though, everything worked out. I still get their flyers and such from time to time on my Facebook page. Some of their stuff looks questionable (dollar signs and stacks of money and whatnot next to the church photo), but I know God's still working on everybody so I just click "Like" and pray for 'em.

So if this lady was one of the Dukes's friends, it made sense that she might be a little off. Seeing as I'm seventy-five, I gives people a young-and-silly pass until they hit about 50 years old. This woman probably had about ten years or so until hers expired.

Since Rev. Martin didn't seem to have any more words to say to me and I didn't want to say anything I'd have to repent for later, I decided to go on to my vehicle. The daylight hours hadn't changed yet, so we still had a little sun left.

Well, at least she don't hold service too long.

She was waiting at my car with two large suitcases. I smiled at her as I approached the vehicle. She probably tried her best to smile back, but I could see something was keeping her lips tight. And since Angela's car was nowhere in sight, I put two and two together and figured something must have happened between those sisters on the way from Dallas to Peasner.

"We'd better wait for Reverend Martin to help us load these in the back," I suggested real friendly-like, trying to disarm her attitude.

"I can lift them. They aren't very heavy," she said.

Now, like I said, she had to be about 40 so she wasn't no skinny spring chicken. Around that time of age, a woman has to learn her bones and muscles ain't 20 no more. I don't care how much exercisin' and eatin' right you do, it's like driving a manual transmission. Once you hit a certain number, you got to switch gears period, no matter what kind of car you drivin'. But obviously she hadn't learned that 'cause she slung those suitcases in the rear part like she been workin' for American Airlines baggage department.

Then she walked around to the passenger's side like she

just won a medal, but through the tinted windows, I saw her rubbing that right shoulder.

Mmmm hmmm. She gon' learn.

Chapter 3

Once I started up the engine, I just let the music from Crystal Aikin take us on to the hotel because I could tell my guest was exhausted by the way she flopped her head on the headrest as soon as she got fastened in.

"Long day, huh…*Prophetess?*"

"Yes, ma'am. And you can call me Falanda. I respect my elders."

"Mighty fine."

She closed her eyes and I took that as my cue to refrain from any small-talk.

When we got to the hotel only five minutes later, I had to touch her arm to wake her.

She jumped. "Ooh!"

"I'm sorry. Didn't mean to scare you, but we're here."

She stretched a bit. "No. I just don't like to be touched."

"I'll try to remember that." Everybody has their own preferences. I do try to respect them.

Once again, she handled her bags before waiting to see if there was anyone who could help us. She winced a little but kept on pushing herself. I just followed her to the front desk to make sure she got in all right.

"Hello! How can I help you?" a chipper young girl behind the counter asked. She had curly brown hair and cute little horn-rimmed glasses. The artist type. Her nametag read

"Amy."

The evangelist said, "This is a hotel, ain't it?"

"Ummm…yes, ma'am."

Amy looked confused and so did I.

"Then obviously I want my room," my guest smarted-off, her chin raised high.

Ignoring the rudeness, the girl looked at the computer screen. "Okaaay. What's your name?"

"Falanda Shaw-McPherson. *Doctor* Falanda Shaw-McPherson."

My word. Another title?

"Yes, Dr. McPherson. I see your reservation, but it actually starts *tomorrow* night.*"*

I spoke up. "No. We set it for tonight, ma'am. The twenty-third." I pulled up the reservation on my phone and showed it to her across the counter.

She read it. Her eyes got big. Neck got splotchy. "Wow. Yeah. There must have been some kind of computer glitch. We're totally booked tonight—even the smoking rooms. There's a big football—"

"Let me speak to your manager," Falanda cut her off.

"Sure. Just a second."

The girl disappeared behind a partition. A few seconds later, she emerged with a tall man at her side. Despite his height, he had a baby-face, with thick lips and chubby cheeks.

"Hi, I'm Aaron. Amy just told me about the mix-up and I'm so sorry. I cannot apologize enough. Our system went through a reset and we've had nothing but problems since then."

"Yeah? Well you've got a major problem on your hands now!" Falanda raised her voice. "I've been traveling and preaching for the past sixteen hours, and now I don't have a room?"

He sighed, "I am so sorry. I can call my corporate office and ask for—"

"For permission to override?" she interrupted again.

Aaron laughed slightly. "I wish it were that easy. But the fact is we are completely booked up. And it is after 9 p. m. If you'd been able to make it just a little earlier—"

She threw her shoulders back. "For your information, I'm late because my flight was delayed."

"I'm sorry to hear—"

"And even if I had been on time, you didn't have a reservation for me. So what are you going to do to rectify the situation?"

"I can see about getting you a room at another Best Western tonight," he offered.

I asked, "Where at?"

"Our nearest corporate property is in Water Creek," he said.

I knew exactly where that was, and I wouldn't send my enemy's dog to Water Creek—not even for a *sip* of water. I shook my head. "No. We don't want her goin' there."

I didn't want to, but I made Falanda an offer 'cause it was too late for all this arguing. "We can get to the bottom of this tomorrow. But tonight, you can stay at my house since it's empty except for me anyway."

Falanda crossed her arms. "I've got a better idea. How about they're just going to have to kick somebody out of this hotel." She cocked her neck to the side and settled her gaze on the manager.

"Ma'am, that's not possible," Aaron said.

"Oh, yes it is." Her face hardened with fury.

I could feel something had ticked inside her. *This ain't good, Lord.*

And I tell you, Falanda stomped off down the first hall she saw and started bamming on people's doors with the palm of her hand. "Get up! Everybody up! We've got an emergency!" Hollerin' like she done lost her mind. "Up and out! Now!"

I chased after her. "Falanda! *Apostle! Prophetess!* Stop this!"

She made it down about four rooms on both sides before people started poking their heads out the doors.

"What's going on?" one woman asked.

"Is there a fire?" someone else asked, rubbing his eyes with a fist.

Aaron came after us, shaking out his hands at his side. "Everything fine is. I—I mean everything is fine. Go back to your rooms."

"Yes. Go back," I echoed.

"No, it's not! I declare and profess that somebody is coming up out of one of these rooms for the woman of Gawt tonight! In Jesus' name!"

I got between her and the next door down the hallway. Stood there with my hands on my hips and hissed so as only me and her could hear, "He ain't got nothin' to do with you actin' a fool! You in here makin' the church, black folk, and most of all, Jesus look bad up in here."

"Mama B," she said in a threatening tone, "I'm a prophetess, but I *will* get with you."

"You get with *me* and you gon' get *got.*" Lord knows I wasn't gonna fight nobody—but I knew He'd do it for me if she tried to lay a hand on me.

She blew hot breath into my face, but must have decided better than to try to push me aside.

I told her, "Now, these folk made a mistake, plain and simple. They gonna make it up to us one way or another, right Aaron?"

He nodded emphatically. "Yes, ma'am. Certainly."

From the corner of my eye I could see Amy on the telephone. I already knew she was calling the police, and the closest one must have been in the parking lot or something because she was still on the phone when he walked in.

A few more guests had stepped into the corridor by then.

"Ladies, can we continue this discussion at the desk?" Aaron suggested.

"Yes, I agree." I shooed Falanda to go on.

With me and Aaron walking and that police officer standing at the front counter looking at us, Falanda didn't have much of a choice. We made our way back to the desk.

The policeman looked down his nose. "What's the problem?"

"The problem, officer, is that we reserved a room for our guest. She's in town to preach at Mount Zion Missionary Baptist Church, Pastor Ed Phillips," I said because Aaron's face was so red and Falanda's nostrils were furiously wide and Amy's teeth were chattering so, neither of them could have told the story. "However, there was a problem with the reservation and she doesn't have a room."

"But the call was for a disturbance," the policeman said.

Aaron gestured toward Falanda. "She was beating on doors, asking other patrons to leave so she could have a room. *She's* the disturbance."

That part of the story drove the officer to ask Falanda for

her identification.

She whipped it out of her purse and gave it to him with her attitude still intact, flinging that hair like it was actually attached to her scalp. "Do you want to see my reservation?"

He raised his eyebrow. "If I want to see it, I'll ask for it."

He had a little snip in his voice, too. Right then and there, I started silently praying 'cause I knew we was dealin' with two people who was tryin' to both be the boss at the same time. Things could go from bad to worse in a matter of seconds. Especially for Falanda 'cause she sure wasn't the boss of nothin' right now.

The officer gave her license a quick glance. Shined a light on it, I guess just to make sure it wasn't counterfeit, and then gave it back to her. "Looks like you all are going to have to handle this tomorrow. It's a business affair."

"What about my room? The one I paid for?"

Well, technically, the church paid for it.

"Ma'am, they cannot add another room onto the building tonight," the officer snarked.

Now my eyebrows were raised.

Amy said with a quiet voice. "But your friend said you could stay at her house tonight. Right?"

Falanda swiveled her neck around and wagged her finger in Amy's face. "Nobody's talking to you, girl!"

"Miss McPherson, I'm going to have to ask you to leave the premises," the officer said, extending an arm toward the sliding doors.

"How about if I sleep right here on the couch tonight?" Falanda clomped onto the carpeted area and plopped herself down on the lobby's elegant gold and white sofa. "Aaron and Amy can bring me a blanket since they can't find me another room. Standin' there lookin' all useless."

The officer bit his bottom lip like he was trying to keep himself from going off.

Lord, please intervene before this girl gets herself arrested.

"Okay. *Now* I'm going to *tell* you not to come back to this hotel. Ever," the officer upped the ante.

"It's a free country," Falanda said. "You can't forbid me to come here, not without a restraining order."

"I'll be glad to request one," Aaron piped up.

I guess he was trying to jump bad now that he had the officer on his side.

I couldn't take it no more. I snatched Falanda up by her arm, ordered her to get her purse, pulled one of those heavy bags to my car and liked ta threw my *own* shoulder out helping her put her suitcase in the rear quickly.

Falanda flung herself into the passenger's seat.

I opened my side, stuck my head in the car and told her, "Listen here, I don't care how mad you are about this mistake with the reservation, whoever taught you to respect your elders should have also taught you to respect authority, period!"

"That cop is a sell-out," she complained. "He's probably married to a white woman."

"You worryin' 'bout the wrong thing right now. Stay put right here while I go get the other suitcase."

Once I heard her snap her seatbelt on, I marched back into the lobby area. I grabbed the other bag.

"Let me get that for you," the officer said as he reached for the handle.

I jerked it away and said, "Oh, no. I've got it." 'Cause I could see by the smirk on his face that he was itchin' to have more words with Falanda. I really wasn't up to seeing somebody get tasered, plus the church didn't have no budget code for bailing guest ministers out of jail.

Soon as I set that other bag in the car, I took off before the officer could change his mind about letting us go.

And that's when the reality hit me: This woman gonna need a place to stay, not just tonight, but all week seeing as she done got herself kicked out of the only nice hotel in Peasner!

Lord, help me.

Chapter 4

Falanda blew breath out of her nose real hard all the way home. I don't know if she called herself mad at the hotel people, at the police, at me, or all three, but I didn't care 'cause I was mad, too. *Got me out all times of night running interference for her foolishness.*

When we turned on my street, her eyes started squinting, I suppose trying to get a picture of my and Frank's neighborhood in the dark.

"This the white side of town?"

"Mixed."

"Hmph. Looks white to me. You married to a white man?"

"No. But if I was, would it matter?"

"That would be your problem, not mine," she huffed.

I pressed the garage door opener and pulled inside. "Looka here, evangelist prophetess, I don't want no trouble. I got a lot of friends—different colors, different walks of life, different sides of the track. We all get along here."

She leaned up against her door. "I see how you get along with everybody. You got the spirit of sugar-coating."

"The what?!"

"The spirit. Of. Sugar-coating," she repeated real slow, like I can't hear.

I whipped my neck around to her. "What I *got* is common sense enough to know you ain't gonna get your way by

31

bullying people around with a loud mouth and a bad wig. Now, come on in this house and let me show you to your room so we can both repent and go to bed."

"My God, my God," Falanda tsked as she exited the vehicle.

I'mma confess to y'all right now: I spends plenty of time in the Word and plenty of dedicated time in His presence, but when I'm tired and sleepy and irritated and should have been between the sheets forty-five minutes ago, plus I miss my husband...sometimes I have a moment in the flesh. And this sure was one of 'em. *Forgive me, Lord.*

I led her straight to her room. Showed her where the bathroom was, where the towels were, and how to operate the ceiling fan. "Good night, Falanda."

"Mmmm," she grunted.

I had to get down on my knees in my room. "Lord. No." That was all I could say over and over again—just *no*! I done helped a lot of people in my life. Some of 'em was beat down by life, some physically sick, some lost, some too young to know much, and some just slow to catch on to life, period.

But this one here was the kind I didn't fool with—the kind who think they already know it all. Got some kind of titles and certificates they probably paid $39.99 for and printed right off the Internet, and call you everything but a child of God if you twist their name up.

I tried to tell God, "Father, even You don't deal with people who don't want to listen. You stand at the door and knock, and if they don't answer..."

I had to stop right there and ask myself some questions: *What does Jesus do if someone doesn't answer? Does He just walk away? Or does He keep knocking? How many times does*

He knock?

If He does walk away, He's so gracious that I imagine He stops only after He has tried for a long, long time.

So then I started to tell the Father that I was tired of knocking on her door when He reminded me: I hadn't even *started* knocking on Falanda's door in the love of Christ.

Thankfully, my cell phone rang. I normally wouldn't answer it while I was in prayer, but this time I was glad to have an "out" for this particular conversation with the Lord.

Frank's name and number lit up my screen. I swiped my screen to answer. "Hey, Frank."

"Hey, Honey B, sorry to call so late." His voice alone offered a stabilizing comfort.

"No problem. I'm glad to hear your voice." I pushed myself off the floor and into a sitting position on our bed. "I'm still up anyway."

"Why? The revival run long tonight?"

"No. She didn't preach long. But there was a mix-up at the hotel. She didn't have a room, so she's staying with me tonight."

"Well, God worked everything out, right? Just so happens you had an empty house when you needed it," he chirped.

"You don't mind us having another stranger in the house?" I tried to get him to re-think this thing. After all, if my husband happened to say that I couldn't have houseguests, the Lord would surely require that I submit to his leadership. "I know you wasn't too crazy about when I invited Danielle and her kids to stay here for a while. Never know what strangers might do to damage your property, right?"

Come on, honey, pull up one of them "no's" from deep down in your heart.

"B, I trust your judgment. And God's," he backed out of my dilemma without even knowing he was ever in it.

"Okay," I relented. *Why he can't be disagreeable when I need him to be?*

"How's the medical conference going?"

"Fine. The usual. Workshops, free samples. Lots of food. But nothing as good as yours."

"Awww…you're so sweet, Frank Wilson. I miss you already."

"Same here. Wish you had come."

About that time, I was thinking the same thing. I moaned, "Mmmm."

"I've got something for you," he said.

"Really? What?"

"It's a surprise. You'll have to wait until I get back."

I smiled. "Why'd you go and tell me, then? Now I got to wonder about it all week."

He laughed. "Gotta keep you looking forward to my return."

"Oh, I don't need no special surprise to get excited about you coming home. Just you alone is enough."

"That's my woman. I'll call again tomorrow. Love you."

"Love you, too."

Talking to Frank calmed me down quite a bit. He's so kind. Such a good addition to my life.

Unlike my houseguest.

I didn't feel like getting back down on the floor again to talk to the Lord about her. I know praying don't require no certain physical posture, but in this case, I probably needed to lay prostrate, put my nose in the carpet and point my head toward the east to get a full understandin' of how my path was meant to cross with Dr. or Prophetess Falanda's. For all I knew, she might have been a Five-Star General in the Army, too, let her tell it.

All I could tell God that night was, "Lord, You said in Your word that You know our form. You know that we are dust. Thank You for understanding that I'm tired and worn out and maybe not thinking my best right now."

I fell asleep with a peace, believing God would let me get some rest and we could talk about it later.

He musta thought the proper time was the very next morning 'cause as soon as I got up and fixed me a little tea and got in my prayer closet with my journal, two versions of the Bible, and the book on Women of the Bible that I was reading, He took me back 50 years. He reminded me of a lady I knew who was a prophetess at the church I grew up in. Sister Ringleberry. To tell the truth, most of us kids were scared of her, almost as though she were a witch.

But when I got older and would go visit my mother when I was pregnant with my kids, I'd see Sister Ringleberry at the old church. She'd look me in my eye and speak a word of encouragement to me as a young mother, and she spoke a blessing over the children in my womb and the other ones at my hip as time went on.

The more I got to know Sister Ringleberry, the more I realized she knew only what God told her, which was what I needed to know. Her words built me up and I could always match 'em up with the scriptures.

Momma said Sister Ringleberry had warned her to look out for certain things, and every time the warning proved timely and true.

I re-read the scripture in the Bible where it says not to despise prophets, but do test them.

That's when another scripture rang a bell in my head. Over in First Corinthians chapter 13, right before the Bible talks about what love is: patient, kind, gentle and so forth. I re-read those characteristics. Then I skipped up to verses 1-3, where it says that none of the gifts mean anything without love.

I heard a shuffling down the main hall, coming from the guest bedroom.

Falanda opened her door and the sound of the morning news came pouring out. She walked toward me wearing a robe and slippers, stopping at the entrance to the formal living area. "What are you doing up so early?"

I checked the microwave clock: 5:58. "This is late for me, actually. I see you up, too. I can hear you already got the news on."

She shook her head. "I sleep with the TV on twenty-four-hour news."

Why anybody who claimed to have an ear toward God would sleep through a constant stream of information about the enemy's doings was beyond me. Not to mention how she berated Henrietta 'bout her TV watching.

"You still didn't answer my question," she said. "What's the rush to beat the sun up?"

"This is my prayer closet. My dedicated time alone with Him."

She nodded, open-mouthed like she was processing something new. "Oh. I see."

"You're welcome to join me. I was looking at some scriptures about—" *Not now* the Spirit whispered to me.

"About love."

She waved me off. "Naw, me and the Lord got a twenty-four-seven, three-sixty-five relationship. I carry Him with me everywhere. See. What you doin' right there?" She pointed at the table and drew circles in the air with her index finger. "All these books and man-made theories and writing—you can't carry that around with you. *That* will not save you!"

Her voice had slipped down into an almost-male octave. I guess she called herself preaching now.

"You got to have the power source living inside of you. The devil won't wait for you to pull out your Bible, pull out your pen and paper, before he hits you. The Bible says man ought to *always* pray." She threw her hands in the air and turned to go back to the room. "Myyyyyy, my, my, my. My people perish for lack of knowledge." Then she started speaking in tongues as she re-entered the room.

That girl 'bout crazy as a Bessie bug.

"Lord, I can't fool with her," I whispered to him.

He disagreed.

Chapter 5

With prayer, time, and the special education teachers, my little neighbor Jeffrey was coming along just fine in middle school. He was still a little awkward, I could tell from how he talked about things that happened in his classes, but he hadn't had any major meltdowns at school. He even called himself having a crush on a little girl so I knew he was growing up just fine. Apparently, the autism hadn't halted his hormones.

Jeffrey came through the back door as usual that Monday morning, put his backpack down on the floor and sat at the table.

"Morning, Mama B."

"Morning, Jeffrey. You get your homework done last night?"

"Yes, ma'am."

I rustled his hair. "I knew you could do it."

He smiled as he smoothed the spikes back down. "It smells like you made French toast."

"'Cause that's exactly what it is," I confirmed as I set his breakfast on the counter before him.

He got an even bigger smile, with my teasing and all. Then his face morphed into shock mode.

I followed his eyes to the hallway, where Falanda stood, wearing a headscarf and a housecoat.

"Mama B! A stranger!" he shrieked, hopping down off the

stool.

I wasn't sure if Jeffrey was planning to run away or attack Falanda. Sometimes, once he get something planted in his head, it's hard to re-route his thoughts.

"It's okay, Jeffrey. This here is Falanda. She's a guest."

His eyes were still wide with fear.

I put an arm on his shoulder and guided him back to a sitting position. "She's fine."

Then I turned to my visitor. "Falanda, come on in here and meet Jeffrey."

She stood still and scratched her cheek a few times before she followed my directive.

"Jeffrey, this is Miss Falanda. She's preaching at my church this week. Falanda, this is Jeffrey. Lives down the street. He comes over every morning to eat breakfast before school."

As I figured, Jeffrey wouldn't look at her. Eye contact was one of the social fears that the people at the school were working with him on. But under the circumstances—since he was still figuring out how to get past the sudden fear—I knew not to push him at the moment.

Falanda held out her hand. "Hello, Jeffrey."

He muttered "hi" with his eyes still trained on the plate of food.

Her face wrinkled. "Kids sure are disrespectful these days."

"He's not being dis—"

"Well, is he deaf?"

In a soft way, I answered, "No. He's just trying to make sense of everything right now."

"He's slow?"

Jeffrey dropped his fork, abandoned the stool and headed

toward his belongings.

"Jeffrey," I kept my voice steady so as not to send him into a frenzy. "Jeffrey, finish your breakfast."

"I am not hungry." He grabbed his backpack and went out the back door, slamming it shut.

"Didn't you hear me when I told you he wasn't deaf?" I scolded Falanda.

"I was just asking," she said with only a slight note of sympathy.

"You need to watch your mouth," was all I could say at the moment because I needed to fetch Jeffrey before he got too far.

Thank the Lord, he hadn't taken off down the street. He was waiting at the bus stop, which was right in front of my house since his father and I made special arrangements with the school. Jeffrey had set his backpack on the lawn.

As I approached him, I picked it up. "Go ahead and put the satchel on your back, Jeffrey, so the morning dew won't soak through the fabric and get your papers all wet."

Though his face was streaked with anger, he obeyed. He hoisted the straps over his shoulders, then he folded his arms again.

"Jeffrey, that lady doesn't know what she's talking about."

"She said I was deaf and slow."

"You ain't deaf, are you?"

His frown lost some of its intensity. "No. I can hear you."

"Well, if she wasn't right about the first one, she ain't right about the second one, either. You ain't slow, Jeffrey. You right on time to be just who you are. Folks always tryin' to make life into a big competition, but it ain't. All you got to do is run *your* race the best you can. Remember, we talked about this before?" I reminded him of a lesson he'd learned in Vacation

Bible school over the summer. Jeffrey was my special guest at Frank's church. Everyone loved him and begged me to make sure Jeffrey came to as many events as possible.

"But you said she is a preacher," he argued.

"Yes. I did."

"Preachers tell us what God says. Correct?"

For somebody struggling with autism, that Jeffrey sure could come up with some mighty tough questions. "Jeffrey, to tell you the truth, some preachers listen to God more than others."

Jeffrey's faced settled back into its normal posture. "I do not like her, Mama B."

You ain't the only one. "I understand. You don't have to see her any more. I'll make sure of it. You still want your breakfast?"

He nodded.

"Mighty fine. I'll put your sausage between the French toast. Like a sandwich. You wait right here."

I rushed back into the house and made the creation for Jeffrey. I even managed to put a tinge of syrup on the bread so he'd have a little sweetness, but not too much 'cause too much sugar messes with his functioning sometimes.

I heard Falanda's shower water running in the restroom and I wished like the dickens we was back in my old house so I could run in there and flush the toilet and leave her standing in hot water for a second or two.

She got a lot of nerve coming in here treatin' Jeffrey bad.

I went back outside to give Jeffrey his sandwich. We stood together as he chewed. Still pouting.

We waited for the bus. Not a word. Sometimes it be hard to tell with Jeffrey. He don't have a whole lot of words to say.

Lots of times, me and Jeffrey just be sittin' by one another in silent fellowship, and that's fine with both of us.

When the bus came, he said two words that assured me he was back on track for the day. "Thank you."

"You're welcome, Jeffrey. Have a good day."

He didn't say nothin' else, just got on the bus with that blessed twinkle in his eye that tells me every time I see him what a special gift he is from the Lord.

In my heart, I thanked God because even though Falanda's appearance in the hallway and her mean words had thrown him off kilter, it only took him a matter of minutes to simmer down. This was a major accomplishment for Jeffrey.

Matter of fact, this time Jeffrey had beat me getting' back to normal 'cause my emotions were still fired up.

Miss Falanda had come out of the shower by the time I returned to the house. I followed the sound of her voice, which put me back at the guest bedroom door. She was on the phone yapping with somebody, and the conversation wasn't going well. Her voice was about three octaves higher, volume on 8 out of 10.

So I walked away from the door 'cause I didn't want to eavesdrop. Went back to the kitchen.

Well, she musta thought I was still outside with Jeffrey—or maybe she didn't care—either way, the Prophetess let out a river of cusswords that made my ears wish they'd been filled with cotton.

I found myself pounding on the bedroom door. "Please keep it down in there!"

She didn't answer, but I could tell she heard me because she lowered her voice, though the phone conversation continued.

I know one thing: I was ready to put her out my house. I called to the Best Western hotel and talked to the day manager, fellow by the name of Carl Snow. I asked him if they'd straightened things out with Falanda's room and what time she could check back in.

"I'm sorry, ma'am, she's not allowed on the premises. Didn't the officer inform her last night?"

"Well, yes, but she was really tired and upset last night. She didn't mean no harm. It was just a big misunderstanding." I tried to laugh it off.

Carl must didn't see nothing funny 'cause he remained firm. "I'm sorry, but she can't stay here. We've refunded the card for every night including the first one. We do apologize for the mix-up. It may take a few days for the credit to process."

"I see. Thank you for your time."

There was a new Holiday Inn about 30 minutes west. Maybe I could put her up in that one. I was authorized to use the church's credit card, but since the money from Best Western probably wasn't refunded yet, I'd have to use my own Visa because we had a low limit on the church's card.

I didn't mind using mine, though. I was sure that once Pastor and Ophelia got back from their trip, they'd understand what happened and the church would reimburse me. Plus it would mean getting Falanda out of my house, so I was all in.

But just to be in order, I called the authority in place. "Hi, Rev. Martin."

"Morning, Mama B. How are you?"

"I'm blessed. Gotta talk to you about something, though."

"I'm open."

Well, since he put it like that, I had to back up and get

some background information. "Now, you say the Dukes referred you to the evangelist for the revival?"

"Yes, ma'am. She is…really something, huh?"

Something crazy. "No comment on that. But, well, we had a little…incident at the hotel last night, and now she can't stay there no more. Police and the manager done banned her."

"Banned her? What in the world happened?"

"They didn't have her room ready. She pitched a fit and now they don't want her back anymore," I gave him the short version. "Can you believe that?"

"Actually, I can," he fretted.

I wasn't fishing for no gossip, so I left his comment hanging. "Anyhow, Falanda stayed with me last night. The hotel's giving a refund, but it'll take a few days for it to go through. I was thinking I would take her to that new Holiday Inn. I'll charge it to my card and the church can pay me back later if that's all right. But somebody else is gonna have to take her back to the hotel after services 'cause I don't drive far out that late at night. Reckon Angela can give her a ride?"

He didn't say anything.

"You still there, Reverend Martin?"

"Yes, I'm still here. I…I don't think Angela will be giving Minister Falanda any more rides."

"Why not?"

"Well, when Angela picked the minister up at the airport, apparently some comments were made about the vehicle. The evangelist remarked that it wasn't up to par for a woman of God. Said an apostle is due double honor and had no business riding around in a hooptie."

"The nerve!"

"That's the way it is. But I'm just wonderin' out loud, I

mean since she's already at your house and all, if she can stay there for the week."

"Oh no siree," I blurted out much faster than I'd meant to.

He lowered his tone. "Mama B, it would certainly help out the budget for this revival week."

"What you mean, Reverend Martin? The budget's already done." Stuff like this be set long before we even get to the week of the revival.

He chuckled nervously. "Well, after talking to the woman of God just a few minutes ago, it's pretty clear that she was expecting more than what we took up last night in offering."

"Wait—she was talking to *you* a few minutes ago?"

"Yes."

"So *you* the one she cussed out?"

"I'm afraid so."

Well I'll be a monkey's uncle.

Reverend Martin continued, "I don't want to call Pastor and disturb him on his vacation."

"I agree. You probably can't get him anyway on that cruise ship. Plus he left you in charge. You got to handle it the best way you can in his absence."

"I agree."

"So what you gon' do?" I bore into him.

"I'm not sure, Mama B. I'm thinking about ending the revival after tonight."

"How about if *you* just finish it up?" I suggested. "You got the Word in you, too."

He sighed, "I'm praying about it, Mama B. Got to see what the Lord says. I've got to make a decision by tonight. I'd appreciate you praying, too."

"I'm all over it," I assured him. "All over it."

I sent Frank a text message and asked him to pray, too. Of course, he texted back, wanting to make sure I was okay. I sent him a smiley face with a heart so he'd know all was well—we just needed some spiritual intervention, which can be done from anywhere.

With my husband's prayers going up and mine, too, I felt certain the Lord would work this out. This revival would go on one way or another, and Miss Falanda would be a part of church history, never to be called upon by Mt. Zion again to do so much as pray over a plate of chicken in the fellowship hall.

Chapter 6

The Lord knows I don't thrive on strife, but I will confront somebody in love when need be. The problem with me thinkin' about confrontin' Falanda that morning—while she certainly needed an intervention—was I knew I wasn't gonna be coming from a place of love in my heart. I would have been coming from anger. Anger about how she stormed in the church last night, how she acted at the hotel, about what she done to scare Angela away, how she talked to Jeffrey, how she done cussed out Rev. Martin, not to mention how she had disrespected me in my own house. This girl done managed to offend about ten individual people plus the entire Mount Zion body in her first twelve hours at Peasner.

She definitely had some kind of gift.

Even though Falanda was ripe for a good come-to-Jesus meetin', *my* spirit wasn't right to have it out with her just then. So I humbled myself and decided to let the Lord remove whatever He saw in my eye before we started working on the junk in hers.

Tuesday night, we had a much smaller crowd. Word must have been getting around that there wasn't much reviving going on at the revival. Yet, Falanda carried on as though she had a full house. We got more of the same at church, only this time she got to callin' folk out the audience. When Falanda picked on Kizzy—told her she obviously had a spiritual tapeworm that drove her to eat too many fried foods—Clive sprung up off the organ and left us with no music. I heard him tell Rev. Martin after the service that he wasn't playing no more until that woman left.

I told Rev. Martin we'd had enough of Falanda, but he still wouldn't make no hard decision, even after three nights in a row of her declaring us all hell-bound heathens. The way she talked, she would be the only person on earth who was gonna make it in.

I made up in my mind that I wasn't gonna go to no more nights at the revival. I'd take her and pick up her up, that's what was required of me, but I couldn't subject myself to no more unnecessary condemnation.

I had already explained to her that Jeffrey was intimidated by the comments she'd made. We came to an agreement that she wouldn't come into the kitchen until he was gone for school.

Worked out good for everybody. The only thing I had to skirt around was the email I got from Ophelia Tuesday night. Just so happened I was on my phone looking up a recipe when it came through: *B, we're having a wonderful time on the ship. Amazing! How are things at home? How's the revival going? Write me back real quick if you can. Only got about fifteen minutes. Probably my only time to communicate.*

I know it was kind of sneaky, but I waited for about 12 minutes, then I keyed: *Glad trip is wonderful fine. As for revival, it's going along. Love you! –B*

Wednesday, I cleaned up the breakfast dishes, showered and dressed for the day. I put me on a pair of white pants and a fuchsia babydoll shirt with the words "Jesus Is Lord" in rhinestones. I got it from a women's conference a few years ago. Always wore it proudly. And it was my way of ministering the name of Jesus to people while I was serving at the food pantry for a few hours every week.

After getting myself ready for the day, I came back out to find Falanda sitting at my table, thumbing through the Bibles, sitting in *my* prayer closet.

At first, the breath caught in my throat and another surge of anger rose in me. *Lord, is she going through my private stuff?*

But then He answered in my heart and corrected me. Told me she wasn't going through *my* books; she was flipping through *His* books. *His* Word. Even though I might have bought the books at the store, the contents still came from Him.

I chased away that second wave of fury with a deep breath. *Lord, I'm doing this for You.* I took another deep breath. Leaned against the wall. "That red one is King James, of course. My favorite. But I like The Message, too. It's the brown one."

"I've never heard of this version," she said, still eyeing the large print pages. She'd squinched up her nose, wearing that same I-smell-something-bad expression I'd seen the night before at church.

I wished more than anything that her eyeballs would land on a scripture—any scripture—that would convict her of all that mean-spiritedness.

"They don't break up the scriptures one-by-one in The Message, huh?"

"No. It's all explained in context. The scriptures be clumped together-like so we can get a good feel for what it means in today's language."

I sat next to her—next to *my* regular seat in *my own* prayer closet—and started to close up my journal. But I got the notion to keep it open, with my thoughts and all bare, just in case she had a question.

She slammed The Message version shut. "This too much for me, Mama B. Too much compromise." She turned to me, holding the newer version of the Bible in her hand like a tray or a platter. "Don't you think we're doing too much to try to cater to people's whims? I mean, why are we trying to make this holy life so easy for people these days? We've even got this watered-down version of the Bible now."

She dropped my Message Bible on the table.

I waited for a second to see if we was gonna have some lightning strike the table.

But then I remembered His mercy. And how He'd put Falanda in my life this week. I wondered exactly how much He figured I could get accomplished in five days, but I knew immediately that this here—her sitting at my table uninvited— was lesson number one.

Lord, remove the bitterness from me and give me what to say.

I let the words flow out of my mouth real smooth and nice. "Life in Christ is only as hard as we make it. Jesus said His ways are easy, His burdens light."

Falanda smacked. "Well, *my* Bible says that we have to work out our own salvation."

"You know where that scripture is?"

She flinched. "Not exactly, but I know it's in *this* Bible." She pointed at the King James version.

I fanned the pages to this passage of scripture she boldly referenced, though she had no idea of where to find it in His

Word. "It's Philippians 2:12." I pointed at the verse. "Go ahead, read it out loud."

She cleared her throat, pointed the hot pink fingernail of her index finger at the first word, and began reading as though she was standing up at a podium in front of a crowd full of people. "Wherefore, my beloved, as ye have always obeyed, not as in my presence only, but now much more in my absence, work out *your own* salvation with *fear* and *trembling!*"

Then she looked at me like *top that*, so I did.

"Now I'll read the next verse," I said. Then I read in my normal voice, "For it is God which worketh in you both to will and to do of his good pleasure."

"What's that supposed to mean?" Falanda bristled.

"It means it's all about God working in us. His ways, His lovingkindness, and His character...all a part of who He is in us and who we are in Him."

Falanda laughed, "So are you telling me you think people can just walk up in church acting and looking any kind of way and the Lord will still save them?"

"What I'm saying is that you can't clean a fish until you've caught it. We're fishers of men. We draw peoples in by the love, and we got plenty love inside our hearts by the Holy Spirit, Romans 5:5."

She rolled her lips in, then puckered them out again. "I guess you think you're really something with all this exact scripture-quoting. But none of that means anything without power."

"There is no power without love. Well, lemme take that back. There is power—but it ain't none of God's power if it ain't rooted in love." I could have written down about fifteen verses for her to study just then, but I didn't want to slap her with her own ignorance-stick at the moment. That wouldn't be very loving of me, I supposed.

Falanda chewed on her lower lip for a few seconds. "So…what do you think about sin?"

"I think it's terrible."

"Don't you think God's going to punish it?"

"Sin has consequences," I agreed, "but if you're hoping to help people overcome sin, you can't beat them over the head with it. Most of the time, people know they doin' wrong. When you and me minister to people who are down in the pit, we ain't supposed to just stand over the hole and yell down at 'em, tell 'em how ridiculous they are for being down there. That ain't gonna help. We supposed to offer the rope—the way out, the hope in Christ—to pull 'em up."

Falanda shook her head and cried passionately, "I get so frustrated with the saints sometimes. It's like we just continue to live like God doesn't matter. And people like me are warning people, trying to tell them to repent from their wicked ways before it's too late."

As abrasive and wild as she was, I had to give her some credit. Some people too scared to do what they think the Lord is telling them to do. They get a call on their lives to teach, preach, write a book, start a non-profit to help a certain group or whatever, but they sit back on it, too scared to move forward. Not Falanda. She was fearlessly pressing forward in what she actually believed, even if it needed some tweaking.

Yes, Lord, I know that's why I've come into her life.

Falanda continued, "But we just don't *get* it. It's like we're…"

"Sheep?"

She gave me a questioning glance.

"Sheep," I repeated. "Not the brightest animals, I hear. That's why we need a shepherd. And I got news for you—you a sheep, too. None of us perfect. Some of us saved and sanctified and still in the pit 'cause we been freed."

She flicked that hair over her shoulder. "I have to pray about this because honestly, Mama B, sometimes I'm just preaching and teaching and pouring my heart out to people, but they're not listening."

"Yes, please do."

I'm guessing my plea came across too sarcastic because Falanda had to catch herself from rolling her eyes at me.

She breathed in and out. "Woman of God, I was thinking I could really use a little shopping spree. I know this is a small town and all, but by the looks of your little outfit, there must be some good stores around here somewhere. And I'm running low on a few toiletries, too, so I need to visit a dollar store."

Just like that, she'd ended our Bible study lesson, if that's what you could call it. This one here was determined not to let the Word sink in easily if it contradicted the ideas she had done already constructed in her mind.

Chapter 7

The plan was to hit up the mini-mall first so Falanda could do some clothes shopping, then pick up her knick-knacks at the dollar store, which we'd come to on our way back to the house.

Falanda mentioned more than once that she wasn't as "rich" as me, so she didn't want me taking her to places where she couldn't afford to buy one shoe.

"Don't worry. I know places to fit every budget."

The closest mall only had two anchor stores, but there were quite a few smaller chains to choose from. Falanda was, apparently, small enough to wear the biggest in regular sizes yet big enough to wear the smallest size in women's. So she had quite a time in both sections of stores.

As we shopped, she kind of started warming up to me, calling me into the dressing room area so I could critique as she examined herself in the three-way mirror at the end of the section. She'd ask: *What do you think of this shirt? Does this make my hips look big? Which color looks better?* Every time I told her she looked perfectly fine, she snubbed off my comments, saying something negative about herself like, "My momma always said I had a bad shape." She'd stare at her reflection with a downturned mouth.

"No such thing as a bad shape," I told her. "We all fearfully and wonderfully made. God don't hardly do the exact same thing twice."

Still, she wore contempt on her face. She wasn't ready to receive the good things I was telling her about herself.

She settled on purchasing a black skirt and a fuzzy purple sweater. "You like this sweater?" she asked once we were in the checkout line.

"Makes sense to me, since that's the color of royalty."

Falanda made a choking noise in her throat. "Are you always so Mr. Rogers?"

I sucked my neck in. "What's that supposed to mean?"

"Every time I try to tell you what I think, you always have to come back with something positive."

"I *am* a positive person."

"But that's so *fake*."

My mouth slackened at her rudeness. "So you sayin' if I was negative, that would be better?"

"That would be *real*," she stated. "Stop trying to sugar-coat life."

"For your information, my life ain't sugar-coated, it's *Jesus*-coated. And my Bible tells me to *put on* His characteristics. Like most folk, I done been through some stuff in life. But I'd rather think on His goodness than let all the bad things drag me down. It's a choice I make every day." *Just like I'm making the choice not to respond to your rudeness with more rudeness.*

She smacked her lips. "If you say so."

The prophetess paid for her clothing items and we walked back toward the SUV. At the same time, we saw a big brown dog walking toward us. My reaction was to click the button to unlock the doors so we could hop inside before he reached us. I don't do stray dogs.

Falanda, however, flung her bag to her backside so she

could greet the dog wholely. She bent down and held out her arms, even as I was securing myself in the driver's seat.

From the safety of the car, I watched her rub the animal's ears. She cooed, "You're a good boy, aren't you!"

The dog's tail flopped from side to side.

"Here, let me see your tags." She reached under its neck for the collar. Quickly, she swung her purse back around and got her cell phone. She dialed a number.

"Hi. This is Falanda McPherson. I'm in the parking lot near Payless Shoes in Peasner. I've found your dog."

A smile—the only one I'd seen on her face yet—came over her. "Okay. Yes, I'll wait for you."

She walked toward my window, the dog tagging along behind seeing as he was still getting a free massage by Falanda's free hand.

I pressed the button to lower the window. "The owner says she's only about five minutes away."

"Okay."

Falanda waited outside with the dog until its owner, a frail woman in a faded fleece suit, arrived. "Thank you so much! She must have gotten out of the fence after the yard man left."

The dog's tail flipped double-time now that its bread-and-butter had arrived on the scene.

Watching the exchange between Falanda, the dog and the woman, I had to giggle. *Who's Mr. Rogers now?*

When she got back in the car, I said, "That was real nice what you done for the dog."

She clicked her seatbelt. "Animals are helpless. I can't stand to see them abandoned or neglected. They're innocent. Can't speak up for themselves." A pained grimace covered her countenance.

She recovered quickly, saying, "People, especially adults, though...that's a different story. We can go now."

I didn't ask no questions, just thanked the Lord for showing me what I needed to see: There was something in Falanda to work with.

When we got to the smaller store, Falanda quickly gathered the things she needed. We got in line behind two other parties. The first appeared to be a husband and wife. The second, right in front of us, was a young lady with four long, thick French braids that ended in ropes like what I imagined dinosaur tails musta looked like. When I got to examining them visually, it was quite an interesting pattern.

"Excuse me," I said to her.

The girl turned to face me. When she stepped aside, I saw the child in the front part of the basket, his little legs dangling over and swinging happily.

"Your hair sure is fancy."

She smiled. "Thank you." She turned toward the register again.

Something was going wrong up ahead. The cashier had to call for the manager, which caused Falanda to switch her weight from side to side a few times.

The baby in the buggy babbled some kind of baby talk to the young lady. The mother replied, to the baby, "Not now, man-man."

To which he let out a wail that seemed to fill the entire store.

I frowned, knowing whatever he'd gotten upset about was nothing much. He was just putting on a show, seeing as he'd been happy-go-lucky only a few moments earlier.

Falanda looked at me. She shook her head and rolled her

eyes, obviously annoyed at the delay and the baby.

I squeezed past the basket and stood beside the girl so I could see the baby.

He didn't even have any tears. Just fakin' and shakin'. Reminded me of Son cryin' like his life was about to be over on account of a cookie or something. I covered my eyes with both hands and quickly started a game of peek-a-boo.

Oh, that got him. Those four front teeth—two on top and two on the bottom—peeked back at me.

"Peek-a-boo! I see you!" I repeated the simple steps to the game.

This time, he squealed with laughter and his innocent giggle caught on to everyone around us, including the cashier who was still waiting on her manager.

Well, everyone except Falanda.

The young mother took over the game. She'd caught on to the idea that she needed to keep her son's mind off what he didn't have and just interact with him. It's hard being a toddler sometimes, when all you have to communicate with is a few grunts, some hand motions, and a whole bunch of emotions.

The manager finally made it to the register. She turned some kind of key in the machine, pushed a few buttons, and we were on track again. The couple took their receipt, their bags, and shuffled on out the way.

When the young mother got up front, the baby started whining again because he wanted to touch every item the mother put on the counter. From the way he was whining, I could tell he was just sleepy now.

I giggled and nudged her arm. "Sounds like somebody could use a good nap."

"I don't know why he gets like this when he's sleepy. He's

so *bad!*"

"Oh no, honey, he ain't bad. Please don't speak that over him. All little ones get fussy when they're sleepy. But, see, he's really paying attention to what's going on around him. I'd say he's really *smart*—nowhere near bad. Be sure you get him tested for those programs for the smart kids when he starts school."

Her eyes widened. "Wow. I never thought about it like that."

"Well, *I* think he's *bad*, just like you said! He needs to be disciplined now before he ends up in the pen!"

I had to turn around to see who had spoken those evil words. I'd almost forgotten who I brought to the store with me. None other than Falanda, standing there with her hands on her hips.

Well, that's when the sweet young mother turned into a Mama bear. "I know you ain't talkin' to me!"

"You see anybody else around here with a spoiled brat?"

The mother tried to squeeze past me to get at Falanda, but I—perhaps calling myself a peacemaker—literally stood there with my arms out, trying to keep her back.

"You betta be glad this lady's standing here!"

But then Falanda inched closer. "Come on! Don't let *her* stop you!"

Before I knew anything, I was sandwiched between them two. I honestly don't remember who threw the first punch. All I know was I couldn't go nowhere because of the basket. So I just leaned my body over into the basket while them two was tussling. The whole thing was like a nightmare in pieces.

Pushing me back and forth.

One stepped on my foot.

Somebody's arm bumped my head.

An elbow landed on my hip.

Cusswords flying back and forth overhead.

My own voice sounding foreign coming from my mouth.

Falanda musta got hold of the girl's braids. She was pulling so hard, the girl was screaming and about to come flipping over my back.

Oh, Lord, Jesus! Stop this foolishness!

The baby started crying.

"Hey! Let her go!" A male voice came to the rescue. I could feel Falanda slip back. The girl's body returned to her side of the fight. I straightened up.

The mother's face was all scratched up, nose bloodied, hands shaking as she reached for her baby.

Then I looked toward Falanda. Honest to God, I was hoping she'd have a black eye or something, but she didn't have a mark nowhere on her. Matter of fact, her larger-than-life wig was still in place.

That's a shame.

Falanda and the girl was still hurling words, but they was both being held back real good by some men that worked there.

Two officers came rushing in through the front door. All they did was ask the cashier who she'd called about. She pointed and said, "Those three."

"Officer, I—"

"Ma'am, put your hands behind your back," a lady officer instructed me.

"But I wasn't in this fight!"

"Just do as you're told. We're trying to secure the area."

I was in pure shock when that woman slapped those tight cuffs on my wrists. I mean, just the very thought—*me*, Beatrice

Jackson-Wilson—in handcuffs!

"Can you at least get my purse?"

"Yes, ma'am," she replied. I guess I was happy she'd used a teensy bit of respect. "Which one is it?"

"The black and white one."

"No problem."

They didn't ask no questions; they didn't try to figure out who was in the right or who was in the wrong. They just put all four of us, including the baby, in the squad cars and hauled us from the scene straight to the police station.

Chapter 8

Once we got to the station and we all got to give our sides of the story, the officers immediately recognized I was innocent. They walked me back through the station, past the call center cubicles and the interrogation rooms with the glass windows, to the innocent area of the building again.

The lady officer even apologized for the inconvenience. Now, I don't know why she couldn'ta asked me my questions at the store and saved me the humiliation of a ride in the back seat of police car, but I decided to leave well enough alone. She was probably going on the word of the store cashier, who probably couldn't tell exactly what my role had been because of her positioning.

At least that's what I told myself to keep from getting more upset than I already was.

Me in handcuffs? Cold, hard steel on my wrists.

"Is this going to be on my record?" I asked when the officer gave me back my purse.

"No, ma'am. You were never under arrest, only detained."

"Oh. I see. What about the other two?"

"I'm afraid they're not free to leave at this time. They're being processed. The Magistrate Judge should set bail later this evening, no later than tomorrow morning."

My heart felt for the young lady. "What about the baby?"

"Family members came and got him."

I put a hand on my chest. "Thank the Lord."

She nodded respectfully. "Is there someone who can transport you back to your vehicle?"

"I suppose so."

"Great. Feel free to wait here until they arrive." She pointed at the bench beside the water fountain.

"Yes, thank you."

I took a seat and got my cell phone from my purse. My first thought was to call Son, but I just did not feel like hearing his mouth.

Rev. Martin would have to do. I needed to talk to him anyway, seeing as our revival speaker was locked up.

"Hi, Mama B, how are you?"

"Not good. I'm at the police station. Would you mind picking me up?"

"What?! Why are you at the police station?"

"Me and Minister Falanda...she got into a fight at the dollar store. She's in jail. Might not be out till the morning time."

"In jail?"

"That's what I said. Now, I need you to come get me at the jail and take me back to the dollar store on Ramey Avenue, if you don't mind. I'll explain it all to you later."

"Give me fifteen minutes."

Times like those, I didn't want to do nothin' but run home and get in my prayer closet. Just curl up in Abba Father's lap and let Him comfort me. Except I didn't really want Him to soothe me so much as I wanted to ask Him what was He thinking when He brought this woman into my nice, calm, handcuff-free life.

A voice came from overhead. "Well, we meet again. How are you today, ma'am?"

It was that same officer from the Best Western staring down at me. Got a chill up my spine. I held my purse to my stomach. "I'm fine, thank you."

"And your friend?" That smirk snaked across his face again.

Nodding, I replied, "She alright."

"That's good. I hope she got out of town before she caused any more trouble."

"Mmmm." Wasn't no right way to respond without lying or bringing Falanda's whereabouts to his attention. "Have a good one."

"You, too, ma'am."

I looked down at my hands and noticed I'd been squeezing the handles on my purse. *Lord, I know she silly. But please protect her.* I didn't guess officers had much to do with those actually behind bars, but in a city as small as Peasner, no telling who might cross whose path.

Soon as Rev. Martin texted me that he was almost there, I jumped off that wooden bench and headed for the doors. He didn't even have to park. I waved him off before he could do the gentlemanly thing and open the door for me. Instead, I grabbed that door handle and slid right on in by myself. "Let's go."

"Okay."

He checked his mirrors, then drove on with the flow of traffic out of the police station.

"What happened, Mama B?"

"She got into an argument with the lady in front of me. They started fighting. Police came, carted us off, and brought us all here. They let me go 'cause I didn't have nothin' to do with it. But Prophet Falanda and the other girl got to wait until the judge set bail."

"My word! This is crazy! How is she a preacher actin' like that?"

"I can't speak on that. But like I told you last night, we need to either call off the revival or find somebody else to preach."

Rev. Martin shook his head as he turned onto the little stretch of freeway we needed to take to get back to the store.

"You gon' preach?" I pressed.

"Might."

"No reason why you shouldn't. I'll be there to support you."

"I appreciate the vote of confidence, Mama B."

We arrived at the dollar store and he let me out at my car.

"Call Angela and tell her to see about changing Falanda's flight."

"Okay."

As I searched for my keys, Rev. Martin spoke, "I imagine it's been a rough day for you. You should get some rest."

I clutched the keys and unlocked my door. "Not just yet. I got to try and get hold of Apostle Falanda's family so they can bail her out."

"Right. Let me know if you need any help."

"Will do."

Lord knows I tried my best not to let Cynthia Dukes on to exactly why I needed to get in touch with Falanda's family. "We had a situation…we just need to get hold of them."

"Is she okay? Was there an accident?"

"Oh, no. She's perfectly well. Just need to contact her folks. She from Cobble City, right?"

"Yes, but Mama B, you're really starting to scare me. We're the ones who recommended her for the revival, so whatever has happened while she was doing work we set up, we'd really like to know."

The concern in Cynthia's voice was sincere. I suppose she needed to have some idea so she would know not to refer Falanda to nobody else except a counselor. "Cynthia, I'mma tell you like this here: Evangelist Falanda got into an argument at a store. It got real ugly; there was a fight, and she's in jail now. So I need to contact somebody from her family to come bail her out of jail so she can get on back to her hometown as soon as possible."

Cynthia gasped. "What? Fighting? Jail!"

"Yes."

"Goodness, I am so sorry, Mama B. I know Prophetess Falanda has a strong sense of right and wrong and she's very straightforward about her convictions...but fighting at a store?"

"I'm afraid so. But I want her out of that jail as soon as possible." I stopped there, not wanting to add the reason why I felt uneasy about Falanda sitting out her time in a jail where she'd already made an enemy.

"Certainly. Let me call her father in the ministry. I'm sure he can give me a number."

"Thank you. I'll wait for your call."

I set my cell phone down and sank deep into the couch. *Lord Jesus, what a day!*

Suddenly, I felt a ping in my back. Right where one of

them fightin' roosters had jabbed an elbow in my side. I wiggled a little to make sure I was fine. When I felt only a soreness, I settled back into the couch. I'd probably be a little stiff for a few days, but I was fine.

That poor baby in the dollar store, though. Seeing his Momma get beat up. Watchin' all that violence. *Just ugly.* Even though he didn't have words to capture what he'd seen, he had emotions. And sometimes they linger in ways that sneak up on a person years later without them even knowing why. *Lord, please fade that memory from his mind real quick.*

Cynthia called me right back. "I have a number. It's her aunt and she is quite a talker. Apparently her mother has been in prison since Falanda was a teenager."

That news socked me right in my gut. *No wonder Falanda was so sensitive to that lost dog—she knew what it was like to be lost and on your own, too.*

"Okay. Give it to me."

I copied down what Cynthia said. "Got it."

"And Mama B, I'm really so sorry about all of this 'cause…when I talked to the Bishop, he didn't seem surprised."

"Really?"

"I mean, since he is her father in the faith, I thought he might be willing to come to Peasner and see about her. But he said he can't come to her aid *every time* she get in her flesh. He says he's handling her with a long-handled spoon."

"Well if he know she's a loose cannon, why he won't sit her down somewhere till she get delivered or send her on to somebody else who can teach her better?" I blurted out.

Cynthia sighed. "That's a good question."

Well, I didn't want to say no more 'cause I already knew

the answer. Some of these Bishops-for-hire didn't care nothin' 'bout the peoples under them. Long as they got a steady income, the more the merrier. And I don't mean to think bad about men of God, except when they doin' something bad like calling theyself a shepherd over somebody they ain't willin' to go after.

The Good Shepherd goes after *one*. And I imagine if He got a sheep that's especially prone to getting off track, He'd keep an even closer eye on that one—keep it real close.

Cynthia begged, "Let me know if this number doesn't work out. I'll call her home church pastor."

"Surely will."

Soon as I hung up with Cynthia and started dialing the number, I realized I didn't have a name to go with it. "Ummm...hello...my name is Beatrice Wilson. I'm trying to get a hold of Minister Evangelist Falanda McPherson's peoples. Is this her aunt?"

The woman on the other end, she snickered a bit. "Yes, this is Falanda's aunt, Sadie, but I don't know how much of an evangelist *she* is."

By the cracking in her voice, I could tell this woman had to be nearing my age. Too old to be laughing at folk like that.

"Well, we've got a situation. She came to preach a revival at Mt. Zion Missionary Baptist in Peasner, TX."

"In *what*, Texas?"

"Peasner. It's on the other side of Dallas about 30 miles."

"Oh. Never heard of it. So that's where she's been this week? You know, she tries to act funny with us sometimes."

"Yes. Well, anyhow, she got into a scuffle and now she's in jail."

"Paul Jr.! Pick up the phone!" she yelled to someone else.

"I'm bizzz-eee!" a male yelled back.

"They callin' about your sister!"

"Still busy!"

Sadie smacked her lips. "I'm back. Look, whatever she did, I'm sure she can just sit it out."

Somehow, I wasn't mentally prepared for that, but I suppose I should have been after what Paul Jr. said.

She continued, "Falanda's been in trouble all her life. Her going to jail is old news. Fighting, stealing, hot temper—all part of her M-O. She just like her momma. Always has been, just like I knew she would be."

Again, Sadie turned her attention to someone in the house as she screamed profanity while telling someone to shake the handle on the toilet to stop the water from running.

She picked up right where she left off. "The only thing we *do* have a hard time believing about Falanda is this preaching business. So if you want to get her out of jail, knock yourself out. But if I was you, I wouldn't waste my time or my money."

Right then, my heart broke for Falanda. I got a vision in my spirit of a girl sitting on the edge of a bed crying. Grieving her mother's absence. No one to comfort her. Only mean, abusive words that caused her to harden her heart to protect herself.

If this Sadie was the woman that raised her, if this woman had told Falanda since the time she was a young girl how she wasn't ever gonna be anything, no wonder Falanda was such a mess.

"So y'all just done give up on her already, huh?" I asked to be sure.

"We didn't give up on her. She gave up on *herself*. We just waitin' for her to do the big one and get locked up forever."

Right then and there I got it in my heart that whatever God

empowered me to do to prevent the big one, I would.

Don't hold your breath, Aunt Sadie.

Chapter 9

I called back up to the jailhouse two or three times that evening to try to see what was happening with Falanda's case. Found out she wasn't on the docket until the morning.

Wasn't nothing I could do about her situation until the judge set bail, so I commenced to praying for her and turned it over to the Lord.

Around four-thirty I got dressed to go do the one thing my body needed: exercise. Them aches and pains wasn't gonna get no better with me sitting around stressing. I needed to get some circulation in my bones and muscles to head off the after-effects of being thrown smack dab in the middle of a catfight.

Since Ophelia was out of town, Libby had agreed to be my partner in the class. She didn't really have to do much of nothing, but I always liked to have somebody to help me demonstrate the stretches and such.

My Inspiration Perspiration class had been held over for several terms now. We had quite a few regulars, including Danielle. She was another young lady who came from an awful background with questionable influence, especially seeing as her momma gave her the actual government name of "Trouble."

But Danielle had a different reaction than Falanda. She had gone off into a destructive relationship with a man, had four kids out of wedlock, sabotaged her finances and put on a whole lot of extra pounds.

But God! She and the kids had stayed with me and Frank for a spell while Danielle got herself together. Got her job back, got a car, learned how to be a better mother, and even lost some weight.

Just a few months back, she had announced her engagement to a fellow named Steve Riley. Me and Frank ate lunch with them—he a fine, upstanding young man. He wasn't real easy on the eyes, but usually them kind be the best ones.

"Hey, Mama B!" Danielle greeted me as I entered the exercise room. "Check me out!"

She turned to the side and pressed her shirt against her stomach.

"Whooo-oooh! Chile, you done put that pouch in check!"

"I sure have, thanks to you and this exercise class. I'm going to be *on fleek* in my wedding dress!"

"I know that's right!" I high-fived her even though I wasn't quite sure what *on fleek* meant. Almost sounded like a cussword to me.

When I stepped into the room, I noticed the crowd of ladies standing in a circle.

"B!" Libby called to me.

"Huh?"

"Come over here and see this. Is this you?"

I made my way through to the center and one of the class members handed me her cell phone. She pushed an arrow and right before my eyes—there it was! A video tape of Falanda and the young girl fighting, with me booked over into the basket, hollerin' for my life! My mouth fell open 'cause I just couldn't believe somebody had sat there and taped this whole thing instead of tryin' to help! I mean they recorded from the first lick to whoever it was that pulled Falanda off the girl, all the way until the police got there.

And then I read the title of the video at the bottom: Old Lady Trapped in a Fight Between Two Black Chicks! Funniest Video EVER!!!!!

I'd never been so embarrassed in all my life. "Turn it off."

From the crack in my voice, they all knew it was me.

Libby put an arm around me and tilted my head onto her shoulder. "B, what happened? Why didn't you tell me?"

"I was gonna tell you tonight. What happened is exactly what it looks like," I said between sniffs. "Two people got to fighting—one in front of me and the other behind—and I got caught in the middle. It was terrible! Not the least bit funny at all!" Watching the incident play out on screen was even more disturbing than the flash of time it took in real life.

"It sure wasn't," Danielle said. "Don't mind that, Mama B. People are heartless."

"Can we make 'em take it down from the Internet?" Susan, one of my long-time students, asked.

"We can try," Danielle said.

"Well, we'd better get busy askin'. It's already got over two thousand views on YouTube," Susan informed us.

"I'll go to the computer room and go to their site to request removal right now," Danielle volunteered. She set her towel and water bottle against the mirrored wall. "Go ahead and start without me."

"Thank you, sweetheart," I said. I took a deep breath and shook my head clear. "Might as well go ahead and exercise. Sittin' around here mopin' ain't gonna change nothin'." *Lord, I'm gonna keep my mind stayed on you so I can stay in peace, just like You said.*

"Before we get started, I want to offer up a prayer. I want to be clear: this prayer is not mandatory," Libby said with a smirk. "And the class doesn't officially start for two minutes."

Everyone in the class giggled a little. We had done been through a hard time with the program director over the fact that I played gospel music with the matchless name of Jesus in my workouts. No one had left, and this wasn't the first time we'd prayed for someone before or after class. We just had to make an official announcement so no one could say we forced our God on them. To date, no one had refused an approach to the throne.

We all grabbed hands as Libby led us in prayer. "Abba, Father, we come before You because our sister, Your beloved daughter, is feeling quite hurt right now over this filmstrip of people fighting around her online. First, we thank You for protecting her throughout the fight. From the looks of it, she could have been physically hurt, Lord, but she wasn't."

"Yes, Lord," several of us whispered.

I sure did thank Him, too, 'cause from the perspective of whoever was taping the video, I could see now that a lot could have gone wrong real quick. Any one of them racks of candy could have fell over, and I would have been trapped with my belly against that rolling basket. "Thank You, Jesus."

"Second, Lord, we pray for Your comfort for our sister. You told us in Your Word that all things work together for the good of them who love You and are called according to Your purpose. None of this came as a surprise to You, and we take our refuge and our hiding place in Your word.

"Finally, Lord, we ask for favor with the You-Tubing company as we request for them to take down the fight so the enemy's work will not be glorified in the earth. In Jesus' name we pray, Amen."

"Amen," we seconded.

I added, "I want to also pray for the women in the fight, Lord."

All heads bowed again.

"Father, I pray mercy on them. Let this incident be the turning point in their lives, never to return to a jail cell again. In Jesus' name, Amen."

We amened again.

Susan shook her head. "I don't know how you do it, B, but you actually do what the Bible says—pray for those who hurt us."

I winked at her. "They don't call it the good book for nothin'."

Edified by Libby's prayer, I wiped my tears away and called out, "Are you ready to get your praise on through exercise?"

My students roared, "Yes!"

"Let's do it, then, 'cause He's worthy!"

I praised Him through that class, back home again, and right on through the revival service that night as Rev. Martin stood in for our absentee minister.

The only one who seemed a little put-out that Falanda wasn't there was Henrietta. Thanks to the Lord answering our prayers, she had made quite a recovery from that stroke. She had got some cognitive therapy and speech therapy, too. She still had her slip-ups, but that was nothing compared to all that slurring and gibberish she used to utter.

"What you reckon happened to the lady preacher?" Henrietta asked me after service.

I didn't answer that question. I tried to redirect her train of thought. "That Rev. Martin turnin' out to be a fine preacher, don't you think?"

"Naw. He read too much stuff from the Bible."

"You think so?"

"Mmm hmm," she nodded. "What you reckon happened to the lady preacher?"

"I'm not sure. Let's just pray for her."

When Frank called that evening, I gave him the short version of what had happened with me and Falanda. Then I told him about the YouTube video, too. "And they said I was old on the video!"

"Kids," Frank said. "Hopefully YouTube will see Danielle's request soon and remove it. Something like that happened to one of Dr. Franklin's sons. Someone posted a video of the boy drinking alcohol on his 18th birthday. They got it pulled down on the basis that it was showing illegal activity."

"That's good." I didn't tell Frank that two thousand people had already seen it. Wasn't no use in magnifying the problem when I already knew God was gonna take care of it.

So then I had to ask my husband an important question. "Baby, I feel real uncomfortable leaving Falanda in the jail too long. But I don't think her family's going to come see about her."

"B, that's not your problem."

"I know. But I *am* on the hospitality committee. I just want to see her through getting back home and all," I said. "I was thinking, if the bail ain't much, I'd like to get her out come morning."

"But you said yourself, she started the fight," Frank argued.

"I know, I know. I just...want mercy for her."

Frank let out a heavy breath. "Go ahead, Honey B."

"Why you say it like tha-aat?" I singsonged.

"Because I know once you get your heart set on helping somebody, you're going to find a way to do it no matter what. If I say you can't take it from the household budget, you'll set up a stand and have Jeffrey out there with you selling lemonade on the corner."

I laughed because He was right. But I didn't want him to think I wasn't taking him into consideration. "No, Frank. I don't want your 'yes' like that." I swallowed hard. "If you really don't want me to do it, I won't."

Please, Lord, don't let him say no.

"Let's compromise," he offered. "The answer is 'yes' if bail is less than five hundred. Over that, I'm going to have to say no."

"Five hundred dollars is the limit," I recapped.

"Yes," he stated.

I had no idea if five hundred dollars was a reasonable amount to put toward somebody's bail. "Well, if it's more than five hundred, can we put our five hundred toward whatever it is? Maybe I can find someone else who will put in the rest."

Frank laughed. "You sound like Abraham pleading for God to have mercy on Sodom and Gomorrah—talking Him down from fifty to ten good men."

I sighed, glad that Frank wasn't taking it all too seriously.

"B, I love you."

"Love you, too. Thank you for supporting all my rescue missions."

I heard his smile through the phone. "Just call me Tonto."

Chapter 10

Son come calling me first thing in the morning after my prayer time but before I was set to go to the jailhouse. "Mama!"

"Good morning to you, too, Son."

"Mama," he took it down an octave, "is this you on the video?"

"Yes, it's me."

"Those hoodrats in the video could have killed you!"

"No need in callin' folks out they name, Son. Besides, me and the Lord had a good talk about that this morning, so I got to disagree. They can't do nothin' to me that He don't allow. And my time ain't up. So, no, they couldn't have killed me." I tried soothing him with the same words the Lord had spoken to my heart just that very morning.

"Anyway, Danielle workin' on getting YouTube to take it down."

"Even if they take it down, it's still probably been downloaded and reposted a hundred times by now. You pressing charges?" he wanted to know.

"Pressing charges for what—fighting *around* me?"

"For putting the public in danger!"

I waved at the phone. "Naw, boy. Wasn't no real harm done to me or the public. I'm a little sore but I'll be all right. Besides, y'all sit up and watch that kind of stuff on the

YouTube and TV every day. You ask me, more harm being done by Hollywood than what them two did yesterday."

Son went on and on about how wrong the whole thing was. I just let him talk 'cause I could hear the fear in his voice. Can't blame my firstborn son for lookin' out for his mother. That's part of his makeup. He be so dramatic sometimes, though.

I checked my watch. "Well, I got to go now."

"Where are you going?"

"To handle my business in my own life," I answered.

He paused. "Be careful, Mama."

"Don't worry, Son. I'm always in God's hands."

Thankfully, Danielle called me almost as soon as I hung up with Son. She gave me the news that YouTube agreed to take the video down, so I was able to text him, hoping that would ease his fears.

The jailhouse parking lot sure did have a lot of cars parked out there so early. Folk must have a lot to do with the courts and all. I was thankful this would be one of the few times I had interaction with this part of Peasner, TX. With my checkbook in my purse, I walked past the sliding doors and made my way to the clerk's desk.

After waiting for two patrons who had managed to make it there before me, I approached the bench and spoke real soft-like, "Hello. I'm here to see about bailing out Proph...Dr...uh, Falanda McPherson."

The lady, dressed in all black with a wild mange of red hair sprouting above a tiger-print headband, asked, "Do you know her date of birth?" She tapped away at her computer keys.

"I'm afraid not. But can't be too many Falanda's, right?"

She shrugged and gave me a little smile. "That's true."

Then her eyes squinted at the screen. "Falanda McPherson?"

"Yes. Has the judge set the bail yet?"

"No, ma'am. She's been transported to the city hospital."

"The hospital? For what?"

The lady read from the screen, "Looks like injuries suffered in the altercation."

I was just about to tell her that Falanda didn't suffer no injuries in the fight yesterday at the dollar store, but I kept my mouth closed.

"I'm sorry. I can't tell you any more. HIPPA laws," she stated as her lips literally sealed.

I studied the lacquered countertop for a second while this new information swirled through my head. *Maybe Falanda did get popped, but it took a while for the injury to set in. Maybe she had epilepsy or some other disorder that got aggravated with the hair-slinging and all. Or maybe she was just fakin' an injury to get out the jail.* I don't like to think bad thoughts about people, but in this case, Falanda's history didn't leave me much choice.

Humming a prayer, I got on back in my car and headed over to the hospital. I saw one of Frank's doctor friends as I was headed inside.

"Hi! How are you?"

"Oh, I'm blessed, and you?"

"Same here. Frank enjoying the conference?" He held up air-quotes when he said that last word.

I nodded with a smile. "I'm sure he is."

"Be sure and tell him I said hello."

"Sure thing."

Guess I kind of lied because I didn't even remember his name. I knew he was Dr-Somebody-or-another. I try, but I can't keep up with who's who, really. When you get my age, you ain't tryin' to use up all your brain juice tryin' to keep all these peoples' names straight. Long as we treat each with love, that's all really need to be remembered anyhow.

Plus, my mind was on Falanda. I had run through a lot of different scenarios on my way over. Most of 'em I had to rebuke 'cause I was lettin' my imagination wander too far without getting to the bottom of what actually happened.

I stopped at the reception desk. "Hello. I'm here to see Falanda McPherson."

The lady, almost my age, typed and searched the monitor. "She's in I-C-U."

I-C-U?!

"Room 230."

Those three letters ran circles in my mind as my legs carried me to the elevator. *I-C-U?*

I saw my hand reach and press the button next to the number two. Still couldn't believe what I'd heard.

Then, as the elevator started its course, I remembered some conversations I'd had with Frank. He said sometimes people have to be placed in certain parts of the hospital for insurance purposes. Like if the insurance say no to admitting for one thing, they still might say yes to admission for something else with certain kinds of conditions. It's sad, but sometimes doctors have to work the system to get patients the help they need.

Anyway, I calmed myself with thoughts that maybe Falanda wasn't in so bad a condition.

When the elevator stopped at the second floor and the

doors slid open, I stepped off almost tiptoeing. Something about the intensive care unit always made me feel like I needed to be especially quiet.

I followed the signs to room 230. I checked the names on the door just to make sure I was visiting the right person. It wouldn't have surprised me one bit if the lady at the front desk had sent me to the wrong room.

What did surprise me; however, was the condition I found Falanda in when I opened that door.

Machines. A tube going up her nose. Blood caked around her ear. Gauze all around her head. Lips slightly gaped open, showing a space where she was missing a tooth. Her face so swollen I wouldn't have known it was her if I hadn't recognized her distinctive nails. "My God!" I gasped. I stood over her bed in disbelief.

My throat got so thick, breath could hardly pass through. Nausea curled in my stomach. Tears welled up and spilled out of my eyes and onto her white sheets. Though I knew she couldn't hear me, I croaked, "Falanda. Who did this to you?"

Chapter 11

Overcome with emotion, I rushed to the nurses' station demanding an answer from the first person I saw in uniform. "What happened to her?"

"I'm sorry, ma'am, to whom are you referring?" the nurse asked.

I cleared my face and tried to gain control of my voice. "Falanda McPherson."

"Oh." Her lips made a popping sound. "She's state's custody. I can't discuss anything with you unless you're her attorney—are you?"

"No."

"Then I'm going to have to ask you to leave. Inmates can't have visitors. You shouldn't have been allowed in the room in the first place. I'm guessing the officer who was with her must have gone to the restroom."

I reared my head back. "Honey, in the condition Falanda's in, she ain't no risk for runnin' off."

The nurse shrugged in silent agreement. "I'm sorry. I've only been told that she can't have visitors. Is there someone else on the floor you'd like to see?"

I walked away, understanding that she was telling me in so many words to leave.

Soon as I filled my lungs with a breath of fresh air outside the hospital, I started talking to the Lord. Peoples probably thought I was crazy, looking like I was talking to myself, but I didn't care. "Father, I know she got a bad attitude and a misunderstandin' of Your Word, but You put her in my life 'cause You want me to help her, which means You still got a plan, a hope and a future for her. But God, this...I don't know what to call it...*this* is not You."

When I got in the car, I realized I didn't even have words for what I'd seen or how I felt. I didn't know what to pray. I hadn't seen nobody beat that bad since my first cousin, Kenny Ray Nash, got caught in the bed with another man's wife. This the kind of beatin' where somebody kept going long after the mutual combat was over. It's one thing for somebody to shoot from a distance. But when somebody get mad enough to personally beat you within an inch of your life, they got a screw loose on top of hate.

The car became my prayer closet as I prayed in the Spirit, depending on Him to groan and utter the perfect words through my lips of clay.

Next, I called Frank even though I knew he couldn't pick up. I left him a voice message, "Honey, you not gonna believe this. They done beat Falanda to a pulp in that jail. Now she at the hospital in I-C-U. They won't let me see her no more 'cause she still in custody. Call me."

Normally, my next call would have been to Ophelia, but since she was still gone with Pastor, she was off the list.

Lord, what do I do? Who do I tell? What do I tell them? I know He's a God of justice. And He knows what to do.

But I didn't.

As I sat almost frozen in the driver's seat, despite the sun beaming through the windows and shining on my fingers still clenched to the steering wheel, seem like my mind went back to the 1940s and 50s. I was a child back then, but I heard tell of these type of incidents all the time—folks going missing somewhere between the scene of the arrest and the police station. Or peoples going to jail walking perfectly fine, coming out with a permanent limp. And we couldn't ask no questions or the same might happen to us 'cause the only people with power to stop it was part of the problem.

Only thing we could do in terms of legal help was maybe get word to the NAACP or some other organizations in the North, and they might send somebody down to investigate if they could. But even if there was an investigation and some kind of trial, whoever did it usually got found not guilty if the victim was poor or black or both, and the perpetrator was the opposite. We didn't trust no police, no judges, no lawyers, nobody who wasn't broke like us and especially nobody who didn't look like us.

Even when Kenny Ray got whipped by the man, my Aunt Gloreen didn't tell the police who did it. Partly because she knew her son was wrong, but also partly because if the authorities got involved, Kenny Ray might end up on trial later and that woman's husband might end up getting life in prison for something another man would just get a fine for.

So if somebody stole something from somebody's house, we sent word through the neighborhood. And when the truth came out, folks handled it their own way. Might have been a fight or some kind of tit-for-tat retribution, but that was our way.

Right or wrong, we didn't turn our own in.

But when my eyes fell on the dashboard, with its temperature control knob, four sets of air conditioning vents, and even a button for satellite radio, I was quickly reminded that this wasn't the 40s, the 50s, or even the 60s. We were in a whole 'nother century and the officer on my bad list wasn't even white. Yet, that same old sense of fear was stinkin' up my car today.

"God has not given us a spirit of fear, but of power, of love, and a sound mind," I rebuked it with scripture. I knew this issue was all about Falanda, but I wasn't going to be able to help her none if I was clamped up in fear.

With those words, my insides began to thaw out, so I kept speaking, "No weapon formed against me shall prosper. He who dwells in the secret place of the Most High shall abide under the shadow of the Almighty. I will say of the LORD, 'He is my refuge and my fortress: My God; in Him I will trust.'"

As scriptures fluttered up from my heart through my mouth, I began to praise the Lord in advance for whatever plan He had to use for this situation. "God, I bless You because You work all things for the good of those who love you." I suppose this went on for another five minutes or so—however long it took for the Word to overpower that sense of helplessness the enemy tried to drop in my spirit.

A text came in from Frank: *So sorry about minister. Call the one who helped w/problem @ the recreation center. She might point in right direction. If she can't, maybe Michael? Will try to pull strings so you can see her @ hospital. What about her family?*

In reply to his question about Falanda's family, I had typed out the words: *they stupid* on my screen. But it looked so ugly, I couldn't press send. I backspaced and typed instead: *will try them again.*

The number I'd dialed to reach her aunt was still in my phone log. I pressed it and waited for an answer.

"Hello?"

"Hi. Is this Sadie?"

"Yeah. Who's callin'?"

"It's Beatrice Wilson again. We spoke yesterday about Falanda being in jail and—"

"I've told you once before—we don't have *anything* to do with Falanda. Yes, I raised her and her brother when my sister went to the pen, but they're both grown now and I tell him just like I tell her, whatever trouble she's gotten herself into, she can get herself—"

"No, she *can't*!" I stopped her before she said something else silly. "She *cannot* help herself right now. She been beat up! She in the hospital!"

Sadie was quiet for a few seconds. "She's finally done it this time, huh?"

"Done what?"

"Finally bit off more than she could chew. I betcha it happened right after she got out of jail, huh? Serves her right. She always thought she was more than what she was— especially since she got so-called saved. Started acting different and preaching, like she's better than us. Somebody *finally* put that girl in her place. About time."

You know what I was thinking? For all this technology we got—where we can send pictures and papers and money through the Internet—why we can't poke people through the phone? That need to be the next invention.

Lord, help.

"For your information, it did not happen right after she got out of jail. It happened while she was still *in* jail."

"Wait—she got beat up in jail?"

In the background, I heard a man's voice ask, "Who got

beat up in jail?"

"Falanda," she answered him.

I reiterated, "Yes. In jail. They took her to the hospital from the jail."

"What she say happened?"

"She can't say anything. She all bandaged up, wired up to machines. Unconscious."

"So the police beat her up in the jail?" Sadie concluded.

I said, "Ain't no tellin' right now."

The man's voice bellowed, "The police beat up my sister! Gimme the phone!"

There was a small scuffle as they, apparently, argued over who would get to talk to me.

"Hello!" he yelled.

"Yes," I said.

"This Paul Jr. What happened to my sister?"

"I don't rightly know at the moment. All I can tell you is she went into the jail perfectly fine, now she's in I-C-U at the hospital."

"Nu uh! This is wrong! Oooh! Wait till I call my lawyer! Man, I'mma...oooh! Y'all just wait! Whatever town y'all in is gonna be bankrupt once we finish suin' y'all!"

The next voice was Sadie's again. "Beatrice, we are going to fight this. I need to know exactly where my niece is."

Oh, she's a niece now. Lord knows I wanted to say some sideways words to Sadie, but for Falanda's sake I kept them to myself.

I went on and gave Sadie the name and address of the hospital as well as the phone number to the jail. "I'm fixin' to call a local attorney who might be able to help."

"We ain't got no money for lawyers, Beatrice," Sadie

mumbled.

Paul Jr.'s voice jumped in, "Ask her do they have a public defender?"

"Do y'all have a public defender?" Sadie repeated.

"I suppose so, but ain't that for somebody charged with a crime?" I thought out loud.

Sadie rephrased my words. "Public defenders are for criminals, fool. Falanda's not a criminal, she's a preacher."

My, my, my, lips be still.

"Let me take care of a few things at my shop. We'll be in Peasner tomorrow morning," Sadie assured me.

Chapter 12

I'd talked to Jeffrey's father, Michael, about the situation briefly when he came to pick up Jeffrey after school. He told me Peasner police wasn't known for brutality. "They're pretty bad about giving speeding tickets, but that's it."

Michael waved for Jeffrey to walk on down to their home. Then he told me, "Mama B, this could get ugly. For everyone. Police brutality is a hot-button across the country. Cops walk a fine line between protecting the innocent and keeping the upper hand with outlaws. It's a hard job."

"I bet." I had to agree. "I just want to get to the bottom of what happened. If somebody did something wrong, I want them punished. Period."

He snickered. "I wish the law were that simple."

"If it were, you wouldn't have a job, huh?"

He winked at me. "You got me there, Mama B. Let me know if you want me to snoop around and see who can help."

Apparently, Falanda's family had called the city paper and told them something about Falanda being beat up by the police. Now Peasner was buzzing with speculation.

At Thursday night's revival service, Rev. Martin called me up to the front to lead the prayer and give the church an update on Falanda. Folks had already been whispering about it before

Clive started the organ. I didn't see Kizzy nowhere in sight.

Since Frank hadn't been able to get me clearance yet and I was waiting for a return call from the other attorney I knew, I couldn't really tell 'em much more than what they probably already knew.

I stood at the announcement podium and took the microphone from its holder. "Good evening, saints of God."

"Evening."

"I'm sure some of y'all done heard about the unfortunate happenings with our guest minister. Far as I know, she still in intensive care. We waitin' on the lawyers to call back, and her family 'posed to be here tomorrow. Right now, she is in bad shape. But God gave us healing through Jesus, so that's what we gonna pray for her right now. Amen?"

"Amen," everybody said.

Then I seen a hand go up to my right. I glanced over and saw that it belonged to one of Mt. Zion's newer members, Sister Collins. She was one of the misplaced members from Beulah Baptist—next county over—that dispersed when their pastor died and most of the members went on to his son's church.

I swerved around to Rev. Martin.

He shrugged at me, like I was the one in charge.

"Well, we ain't in no schoolhouse, Sister Collins, but I will entertain a few questions so long as they in order," I said.

Sister Collins stood. "Is it true that she was brutalized by the police?"

"We don't know that yet," I answered.

"Then who else could have done it?" she questioned further, her arms folding across her chest.

I answered, "That's what we tryin' to get a understandin'

about."

"How long does it take to get to the truth?" came flying at me from the deacon's bench.

I looked over to see Deacon Smith standing in his pin-striped suit from 1982.

The congregation filled with angry murmurs.

"There's only so much people's gonna talk to me about since I ain't blood kin. Me and my husband been working on some things. My neighbor is a lawyer, too. Today, I just tried to get the ball rolling. When her peoples get here, we ought to have somethin' started. Maybe by then Falanda will wake up and tell us what happened. We gonna pray for her memory and her recovery right now in Jesus' na—"

"What about that video of you fightin', Mama B? What that make the church look like?" Henrietta blurted out.

"For your information, I was *not* fighting. I was in the *middle* of a fight."

"Same thing!" she accused.

Heads turned from side to side, as though the members were asking one another what on earth Henrietta was talking about.

From behind me, I heard Rev. Martin intervening, "All right, all right. That's enough. Let's go ahead and pray."

"I don't want Mike Tyson prayin' over me," Henrietta had her last say.

The microphone flew to my lips. "Did you see me throwin' any punches or chompin' anybody's ear off on that video?"

That tickled the audience, though I hadn't meant for it to be so funny.

Rev. Martin held out his arms and flopped them up and down to calm the crowd. "Um—Mama B, go ahead and pray," he coaxed.

I put Henrietta and her ways out of my mind. "I apologize, everyone. Please forgive me." Then I went and bowed my head real quick and prayed for Falanda, for peace in our community, for justice, and for her family's safe travels."

The revival carried on with Rev. Martin at the head. He assigned one of the deacons to take up the offering, which would have been Rev. Martin's normal role, and then he preached yet another sermon.

He seemed a little less nervous this time. Pastor Phillips would have been proud. I know I was. It's amazing to me how God always raise up somebody else when it's time for the next generation of preachers and teachers and other church workers to go home. He got to, 'cause we all gonna leave here some time.

After dismissal, Henrietta's granddaughter, Queesha, run over to the pew where I was sitting and apologized. "Mama B, it's my fault. My granny got into my phone today and started reading my text messages. Someone had sent me the link to the fight and...I—I'm sorry."

I patted her on the shoulder. "I forgive you, honey. And now you know better."

"Yes, ma'am."

As much as I be wantin' to come down hard on folks, most of the time I can't do it when I remember how soft God's mercy falls on me.

Rev. Martin motioned for me to wait before leaving the sanctuary, so I waited at the back pew for him to finish turning off the equipment and such.

"Mama B, thank you so much. Sounds like this situation with the minister might be bigger than we thought."

"Might be. Might not be. Won't know until she wakes up."

"You think she will?" he asked. "I got a friend who's an orderly at the hospital. He said she looks dead already. Maybe they're just waiting on the family to sign the papers and pull the plug."

"Didn't you just hear me pray for her healing in Christ Jesus?"

"Yes, but—"

"And didn't we just ask the Lord to be glorified in her healing?"

"Well, yes, it's just—"

"Then just stand on the Word and *act* like you believe."

He nodded. "I know, Mama B. It's just that...sometimes...the Lord doesn't heal."

"Oh, He *always* heals. Whether He heal in this life or the next one, you better believe He got the last word. While we be down here mournin' somebody's passin', the angels be rejoicin' over their soul and that old enemy be lookin' silly 'cause he know he can't mess with that person's body no more. It's the devil who loses in the end. Every time. For eternity. Don't you forget that."

He bowed for a moment, then showed me a big smile. "Yes, ma'am."

I wagged my finger at him. "And you tell your friend to stick to moppin' floors. Let the Lord be the judge of when to call somebody home, you hear?"

"Will do, Mama B. Will do."

My mind was racing so till I must have been on autopilot. Instead of walking back to my car and driving on to my house, my feet took the familiar path from the church parking lot to the back door of my old house, where my ex-sister-in-law was living at the time. She had turned out to be a decent tenant, now that we had a third party collecting the rent.

Soon as I walked up the back porch steps, I realized my mistake. But after living in the house for years, I knew she'd probably heard my feet on the deck. I didn't want her scared, thinking somebody was trying to break in, so I rapped on the door. "Ida Mae?"

"Who's there?"

"It's me. B."

She unlocked the door and held it open for me to come inside.

"No, thank you. I was just getting out of church and walked over here by habit. Didn't want you to think no stranger was harassing you, that's all."

"Oh. Okay." She stepped out on the porch.

When I went long periods without seeing Ida Mae, I was always taken aback by how much she looked like Albert—sharp features and creamy brown skin. I wished we had gotten along better so I could hug someone who favored him. Nonetheless, she kept out of my personal space and I kept out of hers, even on that relatively small porch. "Well, since you're here, I might as well ask about the woman in the hospital."

"I imagine we won't know much of nothin' till Falanda wake up and tell us what happened," I said, tiring already of becoming the town herald.

"Well, I heard they—"

"I don't wanna hear nothin' what you heard, Ida Mae, 'cause whoever told you ain't got no more understandin' than the rest of us."

"Talk what you know, B, but the person who told me is Calendria Smoot, and you *know* she know 'cause her boys stay in and out the jail," Ida Mae said sharply.

In the interest of justice, I thought I'd better hear her out. "What he say?"

"He said that another girl told him—you know they keep the mens and the womens separate—but he said somebody told him that Falanda was talkin' a lot of lip to one of the officers in the jail. Said something about a hotel."

Despite the fact that the word had traveled through so many lips, I knew right then there was a bit of truth to it. "What else he say?"

"Nothin'. That's all he know. Said the girl wouldn't tell him any more."

Chapter 13

Me and the Lord sat up and talked for some time Friday morning over tea, a bowl of oatmeal, and the book of Hebrews. Frank and I had studied this book together, actually, and he helped me see some things about God, Jesus, and what happened at the cross that I hadn't seen in all my seventy-five years before our review.

That's the thing about this life in Christ—it never gets old. There's always something more to know about Him, a deeper knowledge, a deeper love. And just when you think He can't get no sweeter, here come His Word sprinklin' more sugar!

Bless Your holy name, Lord!

I read through Hebrews again, taking notes and thinking to myself how much I wish I had known these things earlier—about the new covenant, and how Christ really did pay for our sins at the cross. How all the folks in the Old Testament Bible days had it good, but we got it even better now.

I couldn't help but wonder how much different I would have raised my kids, taught my Sunday school classes and rested in Him if I had been aware. All them years of trying to add to what Jesus did…well, I imagine if there's any gold in them, it'll come through the fire. But all the stuff I did for the wrong reasons and all the time I painted God like the big bad wolf who would attack if they didn't obey—none of that's gonna stand. When I have to give account, I imagine I'm just gonna say, "Lord, I didn't know You very well then."

I was just thankful the Lord left me around long enough to get to see how soft His heart really is toward us. The thing is—it's all there in the Word! I suppose we just thought it was too good to be true at the time.

Thank You, Lord, for revealing Your love to me.

Frank called me before his seminar started that morning. He told me to go register with the hospital chaplain's office. That way I could get access to Falanda for a little time every day, depending on her condition.

"Just ask for Pastor Rip. He'll be expecting you."

"Rip? As in R-I-P?"

Frank confirmed.

I laughed. "That ain't no good name for a somebody tryin' to pray over sick people."

"I know. It's a longstanding joke at the hospital."

"Well, all right. If you say so. And thank you, honey. I can't wait for you to get back Sunday. This week has been nothing short of a bootleg circus!"

"I can't wait to see you, either," Frank said. "I really do hope you like the surprise."

"Dr. Frank Wilson. I do declare, you are trying to make me anxious!"

He kissed me through the phone. "Gotta go. Love you, Honey B."

I laughed, eager to play this game with my husband. "Well, I've got a surprise for you, too."

"Is that so?"

"Mmm hmmm," I said, knowing good and well I didn't bit more have a surprise for him—yet. This man had managed to put a honey-do on my list, even in his absence.

Jeffrey's knock at the back door signaled the close of my conversation with Frank. "Gotta go, honey. My son from down the street is here."

"Okay. Tell him I said hello. And text me around noon or so to let me know about the attorney. If she can't help, we need to move on."

"I agree."

We said our lovey-dovey goodbyes as I let Jeffrey in the house and led him to the kitchen for breakfast. "Morning, Jeffrey."

"Good morning, Mama B."

As he walked to his usual stool, I noticed in that instant how much taller he had gotten in just the last few months. It's like that with kids. You turn around and the next thing you know, they done shot up an inch.

Jeffrey wasn't a big fan of oatmeal, so I had to load up his serving with raisins and dried cranberries. "This right here will stick to your ribs, Jeffrey."

He looked down at his chest, horrified.

"Not from the outside. It'll stick from the *inside*, after you eat it."

"Oh," Jeffrey laughed at himself.

Once again, I had to thank the Lord. Jeffrey was beginning to pick up on subtle humor here and there.

I started loading the dishwasher and straightening up, still chatting with Jeffrey in our friendly way.

"Where is the mean lady?" he asked.

I hung the dishtowel on the oven door's handle. "Oh, Jeffrey. She's in the hospital."

Surprised, he asked, "What happened to her?"

"Looks like she had a problem with somebody."

"Maybe she was mean to them and they got mad," he suggested.

I sighed. "Maybe she was, Jeffrey. Maybe she was."

Soon as I got Jeffrey off to school, I headed to that mediator's office. Decided I wasn't gonna wait on her no more. If Ms. Gamez couldn't help Falanda, we'd have to move on, just like my husband said. When I got to the door of her old Victorian building, I saw right on the door why she hadn't called me back. There was a picture of her, swaddling a baby, with a man next to her. Beneath the picture were the words: *Office closed through Thanksgiving! Will be returning calls and emails within 48 hours.*

I had to smile at the picture of the family. That little pink butterball was more than enough reason for her to take some time off as well as take her time getting back to folks. She had her priorities right. "God, bless her and her family," I prayed as I walked down the steps and back to my Mini Cooper.

My next stop, of course, was the hospital to meet Pastor Rip. That same receptionist called for him to come out and meet me. I promise you, Pastor Rip looked just like Tim Conway on the Carol Burnett show. Had to stop myself from looking down at his feet to see if he was shuffling! *Whoo, Lord, don't let me laugh at him! That Carol Burnett Show was something else!*

"Hi! You must be Dr. Wilson's wife?" He extended his hand.

"Yes. Beatrice." I shook it.

"Wonderful! Come on into my office," he said, leading the

way.

I followed him down the main corridor to a side hallway and into his small room just past the chapel. He had several scripture plaques along the walls. So many that I can't imagine he bought them all. People probably gave them to him over the years, thinking a pastor can't have too much of the Word to look at all day.

He sat at his small varnished desk; I settled in the guest's chair, folding hands across my handbag.

"Frank tells me you have a friend...oh"—he tipped his head toward the door—"close that, please."

I obliged.

"You have a friend in custody in I-C-U?"

"Yes. Her family is coming, but I think her situation is pretty dire . I'd like to sit with her."

Pastor Rip opened a side drawer and produced a form. He checked off a few boxes, scribbled a signature, and said, "Perfect. I'll take you to the administrative office. They'll create a picture ID. You—my team—will be allowed a few hours a day with her."

"Of course," I agreed.

I let him walk me through the process, glad no one asked any questions. Whether they were respectful of him, my husband or both, I thanked God for the favor to be able to get in and see her.

And I wasn't a minute too early. When I got to her room after showing my ID to the nurse and the security guard, I walked in to find two nurses having a time with her.

"Miss McPherson, you're okay. You're fine," one of them was trying to tell her, but Falanda continued to flail her arms and pull at the tubes.

"Falanda," I spoke, "It's Mama B. From the church. You're fine."

Didn't help none. She was using what little energy she had to come up out of that bed. *Still feisty.*

One of them finally got her left side strapped down, which made it easier for both of them to tackle the right. Subdued by the restraints, Falanda finally gave up and wriggled to a halt. She moaned a few times before slipping back into silence.

The nurses, one male, one female, greeted me breathlessly. He asked who I was.

I flashed my badge, still warm from the laminator. "I'm Beatrice Wilson. Thank you so much for..." I started to say 'taking care of my friend', but that would blow my cover as Pastor Rip's assistant. *I ain't no good at undercover work.* "Thank you for all you do for the patients here."

"Yes, ma'am," he said, acknowledging my position with a nod.

"I see she's moving around. Better than yesterday," I said, fishing for information.

"She's restless," the woman huffed, still catching her breath. "Like she's terrified."

"You don't say?"

"But she's secure." He yanked hard on one of the straps to assure me. "We'll be right outside if you need us. Guard's there, too."

"Thank you. I won't be long."

Them two left out the room. I pulled up a chair next to Falanda's bedside, took my glass tube of blessed oil from the zippered part of my purse, and found a clear spot on her forehead to apply the oil and began praying for her.

I wished I'd had one of my prayer partners with me—

Libby or Ophelia—but since I was the only one with clearance, it would be just me and God on this case.

Chapter 14

When I finished praying, I sat down in the chair and just looked at her. Every so often, Falanda's body would jerk and she'd let out a low groan. I wasn't sure if it was nerves or terror or her coming to. No matter, I personally was frightened to see her like that.

I wasn't in no mood to be scared, though, so I opened up the Bible app Son had put on my phone and started reading Psalm 91 out loud to me and her. Then I scrolled over to Psalm 103. "Bless the Lord, O my soul, and all that is within me bless His holy name. Bless the Lord, O my soul, and forget not all his benefits." I read off the list of His benefits, His characteristics, His loving ways in the rest of the chapter—had me a time in there so until I read both chapters two more times in Falanda's hearing.

One of them nurses come knocking on the door and ask me if everything was okay.

"Oh, yes. I'm just praying the Word over her."

"Yes, ma'am."

I guess Pastor Rip probably didn't pray the same as me. Not that he was wrong in however he prayed, but this was my way. God's Word makes me happy, and happy folk tend to get loud. Now, if they drinking alcohol and they get loud, everybody know that's normal. But I think it's normal to get a little loud when you get drunk off the goodness of God. He sho' nuff worthy!

Falanda lay perfectly still in the bed now. No more nerves twitching.

I reached around the side of my chair and noticed a lever to unlock something or another. When I did, a spring let loose under me and suddenly I was able to rock back and forth.

That was all I needed to get comfortable and start singing. *We've come this far by faith.* Pastor Rip had said I'd have a few hours with her. I planned to use them wisely, to the full.

Must have been on my fourth song or so when a commotion started outside in the hallway.

Angry voices demanded while smaller voices snapped back.

"I'll be right back, Falanda," I told her as though she could hear every word I said.

I snatched the door open, prepared to tell whoever it was outside that room to lower their voices.

A woman with blond-ish hair on top of dark skin pointed at me immediately and asked a nurse, "Then why is *she* in there with her?"

How did I get to be in the middle of their argument?

"She's with the chaplain's office," the nurse replied.

The security guard was reading through some paper or another.

By the fleshy cheeks and thin nose, I took it that the woman must have been Sadie and the short man with the cornrows and hoop earrings standing next to her must have been Paul Jr. When he looked at me head-on, his bushy brows and doe-like brown eyes confirmed my suspicion. These was Falanda's kinfolk.

I wasn't sure about the third party, a man wearing a brown

church suit with white alligator shoes.

With poked out lips, the guard handed the papers to the man in the suit. "You've got ten minutes with your client. And this will be your only visit."

Sadie, Paul Jr., and the man I assumed was their attorney entered the room and quickly approached the bed. I stood back as they took her in for the first time.

"Falanda!" Sadie said as she held her niece's hand. "Look what they've done to you!"

Immediately, the attorney started taking pictures of Falanda with his cell phone. "This is preposterous! I'm calling the local media. They'll do a story. Maybe it will get picked up by CNN. We need some outside pressure in this little town."

Paul Jr. slapped his fist into his palm. "I bet not run into the person who did it." He started doing muscle poses like the Incredible Hulk. Made me think maybe he was gonna do something silly like punch a hole in the wall.

"Uh, Paul Jr., is it?"

Nostrils flared, he asked, "How you know my name?"

I met them at Falanda's side. "I'm Beatrice Wilson. I'm the one who called you two on the phone."

"But I thought you were with the chaplain," the professional man stated.

"I am. I'm also on the hospitality committee at the church where she was preaching. Like you said, it's a small town."

Sadie introduced me to the lawyer, named Rodell Atkins. Said he was in his assessment phase. He asked me to tell everything I knew and I told him, starting back when Falanda first got into the argument at the Best Western to the incident at the dollar store, until when she got into the police car perfectly healthy and now this.

Toward the end of my recounting, Falanda got the rumbles again.

Sadie patted Falanda's hands. "Falanda, can you hear us? Can you say something? Can you pinch my hand—anything?"

"She's resting," I said. "She building back up, though."

"No, she's not!" Sadie protested. "Look at her! Her face is as big as a pumpkin! She's almost dead! And if she does wake up, she'll probably be a vegetable!"

I tell you, I liked ta put my hand over her mouth to stop her from speaking all those ungodly curses after all the Word I had just sent to work in the spirit realm. "Sadie! You got to stop this. Falanda is a woman of God. We got to have faith for her right now 'cause she can't do it for herself."

Paul Jr. informed us, "I ain't waitin' on God. I'm gonna call my cousin, Bryson Jennings. He work for E-S-P-N!"

Me and the lawyer looked at Paul Jr. like he was crazy, so I went ahead and asked the question, "What he gon' do?"

"He gon' call Al Sharpton, that's what he gon' do! We need somebody to come expose this white police brutality!"

"Well, I hate to burst your bubble, but the police officer Falanda had the problems with wasn't white. He was black—and we still don't exactly know what he got to do with her condition."

"Did you get the name of the officer?" Mr. Atkins asked.

"No."

"Could you identify him if you saw him?"

"Yes."

"Then we need to get to the police station. Now."

I nodded. "Okay." Looking down at Falanda, I said, "I'll be back later."

Sadie's face ground down to a frown and said to me, "She

can't hear you."

"You don't know that."

Chapter 15

One of the other benefits to a small town was the small police force. All the officers' pictures were displayed in the front hallway. Mr. Atkins stood right next to me—watching my eyeballs!—as I searched for the one.

Wasn't but three black officers on the force, so I found him pretty quickly. Officer Calvin Butler. Appeared all nice and smiley on his picture with the flag, but I'd seen him get real ugly. And maybe Falanda had seen him at his worst.

We walked on into the main area, where the attorney all but demanded a meeting with the chief. He got his meeting, too, behind closed doors.

Sadie, Paul Jr. and I sat waiting outside on one of the benches.

"Wonder how much he gon' sue for?" Paul Jr. asked.

"Whatever it is, it's not enough. I've never seen anyone's face so pummeled," Sadie said, shaking her head.

I was glad to know that she was at least concerned about Falanda's injuries. Paul Jr., on the other hand, kept asking a lot of questions about how much this might all be worth in terms of money.

"If I didn't know any better, I'd think you didn't care two cents about your sister," I finally had to say to him.

"My sister—she my *everything*!" he declared to me.

"Really?"

He placed a hand on his heart. "On my Momma."

"What's that supposed to mean?" I asked.

"It means I swear by my momma, my sister is my *world.*"

"We love Falanda," Sadie seconded.

You know, I really don't like to bring contradictions to ; attention, but these two didn't leave me no choice. "Then how come when I called to tell you she was in jail, ain't nall one of y'all tried to ask how much the bail was? Didn't try to find out if she was hurt. Matter of fact, if I remember correctly, you, Paul Jr., said you was too busy to even get on the phone and discuss your sister. But now that it look like she might be worth some money, y'all wanna rush down here and start suin' folk. Somebody explain that to me."

"Look. She's our family, not yours," Sadie mouthed back. "We don't have to explain anything to you."

"Yeah. What you tryin' to do—say you entitled to some of the money?" Paul Jr. added.

Sadie pursed her lips at me. "You won't be getting a penny of it, I assure you."

"I don't want your money. I got plenty of my own, by the grace of God. I just want y'all to know that Falanda is a minister. She ain't perfect and she got a lot of learning to do, but she does have a heart to do right, and that's a lot more than can be said for a lot of people."

That's when I saw officer Butler come through the doors in plain clothes. I didn't point him out to Falanda's family, though, 'cause in the short small-talk I'd made with them, it was clear that they wasn't processing information right. All their thoughts had to jump through dollar sign hoops first.

"I know what I'm gon' do," Paul Jr. announced to Sadie and me. "I'mma Periscope."

"A what?" Sadie asked.

"I'm calling out for help. On my phone. Tired of sitting here doing nothing. We need some action."

Chile, I hadn't never heard of such a thing as a periscope except to look at the stars and the moon.

All I know is, Paul Jr. started talking into his phone as though he was being interviewed by a news reporter or something. "What up? Yo, this Paul Jr. McPherson, brother to Falanda McPherson, my sister. Right now we in a little old bitty town called Peabody…wait, what is it?"

He turned his phone toward me. I help up my hand. "Don't put me on there!"

"Peasner," Sadie told him.

"Right. Peasner, TX," Paul Jr. continued, reclaiming the spotlight. "My sister went into the jail yesterday, and today she in a hospital. Five-oh tryin' to say she got hurt yesterday, but that ain't true. So we callin' on everybody—Jessie Jackson, Oprah Winfrey, T-I, T.D. Jakes, Barak and Michelle Obama. E'rybody. We need your help 'cause I don't think she gon' make it." Paul Jr. rubbed his eyes. "Here go my auntie. She can tell you more."

Sadie massaged Paul Jr.'s shoulders as she took the phone. "Yes, I'm Falanda's aunt. She's not perfect, but she didn't deserve this. I raised her. She means the world to me. Her name even came from mine and her mother's—Sadie and Marilynn put together."

How you get Falanda out of Sadie and Marilynn?

"My nephew is right. We need help from somebody, anybody. Please. Hear our call."

She gave the device back to Paul Jr. and he put an end to their public cry for help with, "Hit me up, y'all. We need you."

Thank God that's over.

"I'mma put it on Facebook, too," Paul said.

"Now, why would you do that?" I asked him. "All that's gon' do is start the Facebook-funeral. Get folk to saying their two-minute remarks and the person ain't even dead yet, like they did poor Whitney Houston's child."

"Right now, we need all eyes on us. Any way we can get attention, we'll take it," Sadie said.

I sent up my own cry for help to the Lord to save me from all this drama.

By the time Mr. Atkins came out of the meeting, it was nearly the lunch hour. He actually came from out the judge's chamber door instead of the one we'd seen him enter earlier.

"Let's go talk," he said as he breezed past our bench.

Me and Falanda's family followed him back to the parking lot, where Mr. Atkins asked me, "Is there a restaurant nearby where we can speak?"

"Follow me."

I hopped in Frank's Range Rover, which I was driving because I hadn't had time to fill up my tank again.

When I parked at the Denny's, I realized driving Frank's car was a mistake. Paul Jr. remarked, "I guess you weren't lying when you said you didn't need our money."

"Hmph," Sadie said with a judgmental glare. "Rich people are sometimes the greediest people you can meet, though. How do you think they got so rich in the first place?"

"Yeah," he agreed with his aunt.

"I ain't got to justify my blessings to you," I fired back. "Besides, I'm here to talk about Falanda."

Mr. Atkins held the door open for us all, like he didn't give two cents about this neither-here-nor-there conversation those two had started up with me. I was with him—I didn't give *one* cent about it.

After we were seated in a circular booth, Mr. Atkins waited until he could see the coast was clear, no waitresses within hearing distance. He leaned in and we all mimicked his body language.

"Here's what I know. Officer Butler was examined. They took pictures of his hands and arms. No scars, no bruises, not a scratch on him. He's not the one who assaulted Falanda—at least not with his bare hands."

"You think he used a crowbar?" Paul Jr. asked.

"No," the rest of us said in unison.

"Paul Jr., just be quiet," Sadie turned her head and instructed Paul Jr., face-to-face.

He winced with anger but didn't reply verbally.

"Here's the big rub. The police department is still alleging that Falanda's injuries could have been the result of the altercation she had at the dollar store," he said. "That's going to be hard to disprove because often bruising or swelling don't appear immediately after trauma. They even went so far as to insinuate that her darker skin color might have hidden her injuries initially."

"Well, she *is* black as midnight. Just like her mother, unfortunately," Sadie said under her breath. "They gonna use her dark color to their advantage."

"That's not true," I said, willing myself to ignore Sadie's commentary.

"She *is* dark-skinned-ed," Paul Jr. spoke his observation.

"I'm not talking about her skin color. I'm talking about

what the department is saying. I was there—practically *in* the fight. That girl didn't land no licks on Falanda. Her face didn't have one scratch on it."

"Again," Mr. Atkins said, "Scars, scratches, welts—all part of the bruising and swelling process, which can be delayed. That's the story they're sticking to."

Sadie said, "Don't they have cameras in the jail?"

"Their cameras monitor the corridors—not so much the cells. Not all inmates are deemed guilty at the time they're being detained. Because they're awaiting trial or bail, they still have rights to privacy in the restroom, showers, and such. So, no, there's no video within the cells where Falanda was being held."

Video! "What about missing teeth?" I nearly hollered.

He squinted his eyes at me. "Missing teeth?"

I explained, "When Falanda finished the fight, she still had all her teeth. And they wasn't nowhere near loose 'cause she was cussing up a storm after the fight. I distinctly remember her using some words with the letter 'f' in 'em—them words came through loud and clear. But now, she missing one tooth in the front. Ain't no way it got loose and fell out overnight."

He paused, like he was thinking it through. "That might be significant. If only we could prove that she had her teeth after the fight."

"I know how," I told him. "There's a video."

Mr. Atkins nearly jumped out of his seat. "Where is it?"

"Still somewhere on the Internet, I suppose," I suggested, suddenly hoping that the tape I'd wanted taken down was still up for this purpose. "We can look it up on my phone."

I pressed the Safari browser and connected, giving the phone to Mr. Atkins. He asked if I remembered the title the video had been given. I recalled it to the best of my ability. Took him a while, but he finally found it.

We all watched the screen intently, especially when it got to the end. And there was Falanda's nice, bright teeth standing out real stark against her beautiful ebony skin. Wasn't no mistaking her intact grill.

All I could do was laugh inside; that ridiculous video might come in handy after all.

"I'm going to copy and paste this link and send it to my phone, if you don't mind," Mr. Atkins said. "This may be our ace in the hole. I have to go make some phone calls." He stood. "I have everyone's number. I'll be in touch later today."

Sadie and I thanked him for his service.

Paul Jr. rubbed his hands together like a fly. "Oooh! I can't wait for this video to be on the radio!"

Me and Sadie waited for it to hit him how crazy that sounded.

"Oh," he shied back into his chair, "I'm trippin'. Can't nobody see it on the radio."

"I'm glad you figured that out," Sadie said, rolling her eyes and looking back at me. "Miss Wilson, can you help us find a hotel?"

"Be more than happy to."

Since my phone was already out, I showed them the map and the prices of the nice hotel as well as a few motels on the outskirts. Wasn't sure about their budget.

Sadie whistled when she saw the prices. "Sixty-five dollars a night's pretty steep."

"Dang!" from Paul Jr. "This is highway robbery."

Sadie blinked her eyes real big. "We can't afford to stay here."

Sounds like a personal problem to me.

Sadie rubbed her chin, still staring at my phone. "Guess we're going to have to sleep in the car."

"That's fine," Paul Jr. said, "I got my butcher knife."

"Unless you can think of something else," Sadie dry-begged.

No, no, and more no. He had already pushed me to the limit with letting Falanda stay with me. Her family was a different story.

I didn't even let the idea of them staying with me for a few nights enter my thoughts good. I still had the money Frank gave me to resolve the issue with Falanda in my purse. This—being hospitable to her family—was about to take me over the edge. "I can put you up for one night, but that's it," I offered.

Paul Jr. waved me off. "Naw, that's all right. You ain't slick, trying to get some of our settlement."

"For your information, if there is any settlement at all, it will be Falanda's, not yours."

Sadie pressed her index finger on the table. "Falanda knows to put family first."

Lord, I ain't got time to be arguing with these people. "Do you want the hotel room or not?"

"No," Sadie sassed back. "We don't want to owe you anything. Take us to the hospital. We'll handle things from there."

They didn't have to tell me twice. We left our waters in place, I tossed a few dollars on the table for the hospitality, and the three of us walked out before we even ordered food. I had sense enough to know that if they didn't have sixty dollars for a hotel room, they sure didn't have enough to be eating out at some place that didn't have a dollar menu. They wasn't about to stick me with their bill.

I took them right on back to the hospital and left Sadie and Paul Jr. with his butcher knife to make it however they could.

Chapter 16

I slept good that Friday night in my comfortable King sized bed. Well, as good as I could without Frank next to me. *Only one more day until my sweetheart returns.* Pastor and Ophelia wasn't coming back until Monday night. They was gonna spend a night in Miami before coming back to Dallas.

I was hoping the Lord wouldn't get me up and have me go rescue Falanda's people from the parking lot. My wish was granted. There was not one ounce of conviction that came over me, not even after I'd spent the evening closing out the revival at church. All was well with my soul.

And in the morning, the Lord reminded me that Falanda was my concern. I wasn't going to be ugly to her family, but the fact of the matter was: He wanted me working with her.

See, you got to be able to discern the main *a*-ttraction from the smaller *dis*-tractions.

While I was praying and studying at the table Saturday morning, Mr. Atkins texted "call me ASAP" three times. I did consider answering him, but I was too far into prayer to respond. Only reason I knew he'd texted was because my praise music got interrupted by beeps while I was communing with the Lord.

Whatever the issue was would have to wait until it actually was possible for me to return the call.

The reason I couldn't stop praying was because the Lord

had begun to reveal some things to me, things even more important than trying to catch the police department in their lie. All that was gonna come out in the end, anyway.

What He whispered in my heart about Falanda had eternal consequence. I can't tell you no exact words on this one— sometimes you don't know how you know; you just know. Kind of like a baby can't explain that he's hungry and scientists can't figure out how animals and flowers know exactly when to do what they do—it just happens. That's how it is with God sometimes, which is why it's beyond me how anybody in they right mind can deny Him.

Anyhow, I got up off my knees with the understanding that what Falanda needed more than anything was the Word spoken over her. The Word was going to go where no doctor could and rebuild her from the inside out. I was honored that He had chosen me for the job.

What I did have to repent for; however, was the fact that I had let myself get so huffy about her protective attitude that I forgot most people with that shell on been hurt. They had to put it up to keep from getting eaten alive by somebody's abusive words or actions.

Lastly, I had an inkling of a notion to repent for accusing Falanda's family of being a couple of media-hungry vultures.

"Forgive me, Lord. I'm so glad Your Word says You remember that we are dust. Help me to remember it, too."

I got up and dressed so I could start the mission. Me and Libby talked while I was putting on my makeup and fixing my hair.

"You sure I can't get on the staff at the hospital so I can join you?" she asked.

"No. Frank already done got Chaplain Rip to overlook a

few technicalities for me. I don't want to push it."

She sighed. "I suppose so. Good thing prayers ain't limited by time or space. I'll be back home praying while you're at her bedside."

"Thank you so much, Libby. I don't think I tell you enough how much I appreciate you agreeing with me in prayer for all these years. Not everybody got a friend like you."

"Same to you, B. If it wouldn't have been for your prayers, I never would have made it after Peter passed on."

When she said that, for some reason it hit me that one of these days, Libby and I wouldn't have each other no more; somebody got to go on first, unless the Lord come back real soon.

"I love you, my sister."

"Love you, too, B."

Another message came through from Mr. Atkins. This time, I called him back. "This is Beatrice."

"Thank you for calling," he stated flatly.

"I'm so sorry. I was otherwise occupied."

"Well, I suppose it doesn't matter either way. The judge is playing hardball. He still wants someone to post bail, even in light of the circumstances and the video."

"Mmm. How much they set it for?"

"Five hundred."

That's exactly what Frank and I had allotted, but I wasn't ready to offer it up just yet. "Sadie and Paul Jr. prepared to pay?"

"Between me and you, Mrs. Wilson, those two slept out in the parking lot last night. They don't have money for bail and I doubt they'll have money for me, either."

"You think you'll be able to win a case for Falanda so she

can get justice and you can get your payment, too?"

"It's fifty-fifty. The video shows that Falanda was fine after the fight at the store, but the officer we suspect of assaulting her had no physical injuries. We conducted a few interviews with inmates late last night. From what I gather, in addition to the judge's stance, sounds like Ms. McPherson probably got into an altercation with another inmate."

Wouldn't surprise me. "But how could they let one inmate pulverize her? Seem like they ought to be able to rush in there and stop it."

"You'd think so, but that's not always the case. Inmate-on-inmate violence is a fact of life. And, unfortunately, the judge was more convinced of Falanda's explosive temper caught on the video."

That didn't surprise me, either. But something still wasn't setting right with me about all of this. Sounded to me like the police changed up their story once they saw the tape, but I couldn't worry about that right now. "So what happens if I don't post bail?"

"Nothing. She'll stay in custody until she recovers...or not."

"Is there anything else you need from me?"

"No," he said with a question mark in his tone. "I guess I was thinking you were going to post for her."

"Let me ask you this. As long as she's in custody, who's rackin' up her hospital bill?"

"The county."

"Then I'm gonna keep it that way 'cause I know someway somehow, somebody on that end done something wrong. Even though I'm a tax paying citizen and it's coming out of my pocket, too, I still feel like least we can do is foot the tab for now."

"As you wish."

Wasn't no money in it for him. I suppose I can't blame him, seeing as he was in business to make a living. He was doing me a kindness by calling.

Wasn't nothing left for me to do but the will of the Lord for Falanda. He would have to work out the rest later.

I drove on to the hospital with my Bible in hand as well as a CD player and my old "The Bible Experience" CDs. I figured that was the best way to let the Word play even when I was gone. Didn't matter what scriptures was playing, it's all God-breathed, according to the scriptures.

Soon as I stepped out my car, here come Sadie and Paul Jr. hopping out of theirs about three rows over. They musta been waiting for me.

Sadie flagged me down, holding onto the same jacket she'd worn the day before as she fought against the gusty winds. "Did you pay the bail?"

"No," I said.

I promise you, both of them looked like they could have jumped me, standing there in my face.

"Why not?" Paul Jr. questioned. His morning breath nearly knocked me over.

I discreetly put a finger under my nose. "Why didn't *you* pay it?"

"Ugh!" Paul Jr. balled up his fists and slammed them on the hood of Frank's truck.

"Now, you look here! The reason I ain't paid for her to get out is for her own sake. She get released, she gonna end up with a whole lotta medical bills for all this. You gon' help her pay for those, Paul Jr.?"

Sadie rocked her head from side to side, "We're not worrying about those bills! As soon as she wins her case, Falanda will have enough to buy this raggedy hospital!"

Paul Jr. cheered, "That's real talk!"

"You wouldn't know real talk if it gave you a popsicle!"

Okay, Lord, put a muzzle on my tongue. I got to use it in a few minutes for Falanda's good.

Those two were suddenly silent.

A hand touched my shoulder. "Everything all right here, Mrs. Wilson?"

I looked to my side and saw Pastor Rip standing there. "Everything's fine. This is Falanda McPherson's family."

"We want to see her, doc," Paul Jr. spoke.

"Oh, I'm not a doctor. I'm the Chaplain, Mrs. Wilson's supervisor."

"Can you get us in to see her?" Sadie asked.

"I'm afraid not," Pastor Rip said. "Security, you know."

Sadie fumed. "Then at least give her a message, since it may be the last time she hears our names."

"Certainly." The pastor zipped out a notepad and pen.

"Tell her Sadie says to keep fighting…but stop fighting so she won't end up in this kind of trouble again. She's too old for this. Tell her she don't want to end up like her mother."

Paul Jr. added, "And from me, just tell her to remember me when she come up."

I could not believe the chaplain sat there and took dictation for that mess. He tore the paper off and gave it to me. "Beatrice will get a chance to see her before I do. She can give her the messages."

I wish I would. Chile, I followed him on into the building and threw that paper into the first trashcan I saw.

123

And every word I spoke to Falanda that morning was filled with love and power and strength for her body and her mind. Her face had gone down even more and she was looking better already, though the nurse said she still hadn't done more than the same groaning she'd done since she got to the hospital.

Couldn't let that report phase me, though. I kept right on praying and believing for her, strengthened all the more with the knowledge that Libby was probably praying at that same moment.

In the midst of my praying and reading scriptures and putting oil on Falanda's forehead and feet to signify her whole body being healed, I realized that not paying her bail had kept her family's evil, selfish words from contaminating the atmosphere. The longer they stayed out, the better. God set up holy ground for her real good.

My hours with her was nearing to a close when I started singing *We Come This Far by Faith* again. One of the nurse's assistants had come in to change her IV bag. I knew better than to ask specific questions since they were forbidden to answer them by law, so I just smiled as she did her job.

Kept on singing, "We've come this far by faith."

And when I got to the chorus line, "Oh, oh-oh-oh, oh-oh-oh, can't turn around..." that's when Falanda started her groaning, only in a steadier tone this time.

The assistant said, "Better go get some help in case she starts thrashing again."

"Wait," I stopped her. I leaned over into Falanda's ear. "Oh, oh-oh..."

"Oh, oh-oh-oh," Falanda managed to mumble—on key!—despite her tubes.

I clapped and gave God a fist-bump. "Honey, she ain't

thrashin', she singin'!"

I knew right then the Word was already mendin' on Falanda deep down inside.

Chapter 17

Since I knew for sure that Falanda could hear, I left instructions for the nurses to keep the Word flowing from those CDs all day and all night. The Psalms alone would take hours, and that's a beautiful place to be in the Bible.

I rushed out to tell Falanda's family the good news, but they was gone. I sent Mr. Atkins a text so he'd know Falanda was coming through. He sent me back a note: *I'm off the case. Family fired me.*

"Hmph. They did you a favor," I spoke to the screen.

Because I know it's right to let folks know what's going on with their kin, I went ahead and called Sadie.

She answered with a snappy, "Yeah?"

"I just wanted you to know, Falanda's made a turn for the better," I said.

I heard Paul Jr.'s voice in the background asking what I'd said.

"Falanda doin' a little better, but she a long way from being out of the woods yet," Sadie added to my report.

"That ain't what I said at all," I corrected Sadie.

"You know what? You got a lot of nerve trying to tell *me* about *my* family," she muttered real low. "Falanda's mother is crazy and in the pen, her Daddy was an alcoholic, her grandmother—my mother—died of lung cancer at the age of forty-six, and my Daddy shot a county sheriff *for real*. We got a lot of bad blood in us. She probably ain't gonna make it, so there's no use in us getting all excited."

"Well, I believe Falanda's got the blood of Christ going for her—He is the only blood that matter," I snapped back.

"You think you better than us?" Sadie asked.

"She ain't better than nobody!" came Paul Jr.'s unwarranted backseat opinion.

"No. But I *know* better. And I *believe* better, by the grace of God. And that's why stuff works out for my good. You can have it that way, too, if you turn from the old you and put your faith in *Jesus* rather than the folk that came before you. We all gets our own individual opportunity to believe."

"Whatever," Sadie tsked. "Falanda comes from bad stock."

"Sadie, if you want to drag that baggage in your little red wagon all your life, that's your choice. Falanda don't have to do it, too."

"I don't think she'll be doing much of anything after this," Sadie cursed. "If she *does* make it through, she'll probably be in a nursing home forever, not even knowing her own name."

"I rebuke those words in Jesus's name!"

"Ugh!" Sadie made a high-pitched, tortured sound. "I got to go."

"I know you do, 'cause that's what happens when I resist you." I gave her a personalized version of James 4:7.

"Bye, Mrs. Wilson. We're headin' back to Cobble City. Don't call us anymore."

"Don't worry. I won't."

When I hung up with that woman, I asked the Lord to search my heart and let me know if I'd said anything wrong. When the search came up empty, I realized that I had done the right thing by Falanda and by His word. The Bible says the things of God are foolishness to people in the world. They blinded by the enemy. They can't make sense of the things of God—it's just like I'm speaking a foreign language to them.

I'd told Sadie as much as I could about the Lord in the time I had. Whether or not she ever believed was out of my control, but I wasn't gonna let her mess up somebody else while she was trying to figure out her own salvation.

With Sadie and Paul Jr. clear out my mind, I must have hummed Falanda's deliverance tune a hundred times that day—from doing the laundry to helping with inventory at the food pantry alongside Libby. I went ahead and washed the sheets in the room Falanda was using and stacked all her stuff up in a corner for whenever she was released from the hospital.

Then I went and picked up a little something so I could keep my end of the "surprise" for Frank.

The fact that he was coming home the next day plus the joy of hearing Falanda's voice in tune with the words of that old song had me on cloud nine. I called everyone on my regular list and caught them up-to-speed on how good God was showing Himself to be in this situation. Son said he was just glad he couldn't find the video anywhere. My daughter, Debra Kay, was thinking maybe it would be best if we moved Falanda to a hospital in another city where that officer couldn't get to her.

"Don't worry. God's been taking good care of her," I told Debra Kay. With that, I was sure my oldest girl would spread the word to all her siblings that all was working out well.

Libby told me to make sure I read First, Second, and Third John to Falanda so she could hear about life in Christ. "From what you told me, B, I think she need a whole new mind about Jesus."

"Yep," I agreed. And I'm glad to share the good news with her."

Frank and I talked that evening, too. He was elated about Falanda's impending recovery. "That's awesome. Singing is a good sign for a full recovery."

"Amen and it is so!"

We confirmed the details of his incoming flight. After we said our love-yous and hung up, I could hardly sleep that night. So I didn't. I got up and went to Frank's study. He got a lot of books in there on life in Christ. I found a few that I thought might be helpful to Falanda. And, even then—before she was all the way back to herself—I started praying about her future.

Just landed.

Them two texted words send my heart thumping: He's-home, he's-home, he's-home.

Ok. I'm waiting at baggage claim.

I felt like a kindergartner waiting for the man at the five-and-dime to hand me a windmill cookie! When my Frank finally burst through the turnstile, I rushed to greet him. He set his briefcase down and hugged me. To my embarrassment, he lifted and twirled me around like we was somewhere in our 20s.

"Frank Wilson, you better put me down; don't you gon' need an ice pack!" I slapped his arm slightly, knowing his muscular arms could handle a splat or two.

He kissed me and then let my feet touch the ground again. "Spent a lot of time in the gym during the week."

"Uh huh," I teased.

He picked up his satchel again. I clasped his free hand and

walked toward the baggage mills. Several other reunions took place around us, friends and family members happy to see one another again.

After a little catching up, I bugged, "So, what'd you get me?"

"What'd you get *me*?" Frank played along.

"You first."

"Ladies first. Always."

I batted my lashes. "My gift to you is at home."

He shook his head. "You got me." He flipped open his briefcase and produced a book with a box of crayons. "Taa-daa!"

Trying to hide the disappointment taking over my facial expression, I gazed down at this so-called surprise. "Uh huh. I see." I flipped through to the first pages and saw that this was not only a book with no words, it had no colors, either.

"It's a coloring book," Frank announced with glee.

"Is this for me or one of the grands?"

"It's for *you*. It's an *adult* coloring book. When I left, you were talking about how you wanted to be creative but you really didn't have time to fit anything else into your twenty-four hours. They had a session on stress-relief at the seminar. I got to thinking a coloring book would be perfect for you."

"Mmmm," I held back, examining the back cover and spine of this overgrown toy.

"You don't like it?"

"Oh, it's fine," I recovered quickly and tiptoed to give him another kiss. "I guess I was thinking you'd get me, you know, a souvenir from *Chicago*."

"This *is* from Chicago." He took the book from my hand and turned to pages he had obviously contemplated before now. "See, this one is the state flower, the violet. And here's a Cardinal, the state bird. This one's a beautiful landscape…" he went on and on.

"Well, okay," I stopped him and reclaimed the book, closing it at once and stuffing it into my purse along with the crayons. "I do appreciate the thought."

That much was entirely true.

Once we got his bags and found the Range Rover in the garage, Frank took the wheel. It sure was nice to be back in the passenger's seat, I don't care what them women's lib folks say.

We stopped and got dinner at one of his favorite seafood restaurants, Dallas, which was a rare treat. He ordered a grilled salmon and goat cheese salad. I had a blackened tilapia salad. Since the weather was nice, we sat outside on the patio and enjoyed each other's company, watching the traffic build on Jefferson Blvd. Frank told me how this area, Bishop Arts, was being restructured, though the town retained a lot of its old flavor. I enjoyed the atmosphere, the fresh breeze, the small, round tables covered with a bright mosaic of smooth, colored glass.

When our food arrived, Frank prayed the blessing. To tell the truth, we took so many bite-fulls off each other's plates, might as well have mixed both the salads together. Our conversation was cheerful, even a little flirty, until we started talking about Falanda.

"You be sure and repay the favor to Pastor Rip when you get a chance. If it wasn't for him letting me in there with the Word, Falanda might be gone already."

Frank raised an eyebrow. "What makes you think Rip isn't the one who owed *me* a favor?"

"Well, excuse me."

"I'm only saying that we all look out for one another. When his daughter was diagnosed with cervical cancer, I got her an appointment with a specialist who *stays* booked three months out—a colleague I let beat me at a game of golf, once." He laughed.

"It certainly pays to be kind to people," I said.

He asked me some questions about her color, about her heart rate, the numbers on the machine and such, but I couldn't remember none of that doctor-y stuff. "You going back to the hospital tomorrow?"

"Right after church."

"I'll go with you," Frank offered. "I won't break any rules by trying to follow you into the room, but I'll tell you what to look for and maybe we can figure out some things together."

"Sounds like a plan."

When our waiter came back, he asked, "Were you all saving room for dessert?"

Frank reached for the menu.

"Oh, no," I stopped him. "We've got dessert at home."

"No problem." The man laughed. "I'll bring out the check."

When the waiter walked away, I scolded, "Frank Wilson, I do declare. You done made me spoil my surprise."

My husband got a wide grin on his lips. "Might as well tell me."

I huffed, but I couldn't refuse him. "An iced lemon pound cake."

"I hope you made another one for yourself 'cause that first pan is all mine."

I shook my head. "You and that sweet tooth." But I suppose it fits him well 'cause he one of the sweetest people I know.

Chapter 18

Frank and I dressed in matching colors for Sunday service. I wore a purple skirt and blouse. He wore black pants with a purple shirt and a purple with silver necktie. Seeing as we were worshipping at Frank's church, we were almost overdressed.

They had a new assistant pastor they was tryin' to break in. Young, handsome man by the name of Matthew Withers. Probably in his late 40s. He wasn't up to preachin' the main sermon yet, but they let him lead the long prayer.

I smiled at him, thinking of Rev. Martin and how far he had come just this week alone. He needed the practice, and all these things that had transpired allowed him the chance to get more comfortable behind the podium. It also gave the members a chance to see someone they knew other than Pastor Phillips up there. I knew for a fact one of the reasons Pastor hadn't involved Rev. Martin more was because Rev. Martin was single.

He'd been married once before. Wife ran off with their son's teacher. It was the scandal of Peasner for a while. Probably confused the child more than anything. But that was more than twenty years ago. Rev. Martin had brought a few women to church over the years. Matter of fact, I think every one of us on the Mother's board had tried to set him up at least once. Nothing ever panned out, though.

Ophelia said she wished Rev. Martin would get married so

he'd quit bothering Pastor Phillips so much. "Chile, I had to give him a cut-off time for calling the house. He need a wife *and* a life!"

After service at Frank's church—well, let me rephrase that. After service at *our* church, we drove on to the hospital as we'd planned. When we got off the elevator on the second floor, Frank reminded me to take pictures of the machines and text them to him right away so he could tell me exactly what to look for.

"Got it."

I showed my badge to the nurse, though she went ahead and waved me on without taking a close look.

Her guard must have been on break as well—or either she was still strapped to the bed.

I reached into my purse to pull out my phone so I could fill Frank in. But when I opened the door, I immediately knew the plan was off.

There was Falanda in bed—her body tilted up! Though her eyes were closed and her head was still bandaged, I saw no tube in her mouth, no restraints on her arms, no waste collection bag hanging off the side of her rails.

Cautiously, I crept to her side. *Color looking better. Face less swollen. Praise the Lord!*

I barely stroked her arm, whispering, "Falanda?"

She jumped like the dickens and shrieked, "Ooh!"

I jerked my hand back. "I'm sorry. I didn't mean to scare you."

Seemed like it took all the energy she had to open her eyelids for a moment and get a look at me. She closed them again. "I told you, I don't like people touching me."

She recognized me! More importantly, she *remembered*!

Despite the joy bells ringing in my soul, I managed to whisper, "I don't want to overwhelm you. You need your rest. Just...we're so happy you—"

"We?" she croaked.

"We. My husband and I. My friends and family."

"*My* family?" she gasped.

"Yes, they did come down. Sadie and Paul Jr. Jr. stayed for a while." I thought I'd managed to tell the truth without discouraging her.

She sighed. Licked her lips. "They left."

"Yes. They went on back."

The phone buzzed in my hand. Frank texted a single question mark.

I replied: *She's up!*

Unsure if Falanda had drifted back to sleep, I waited for her to say something else. I wanted to know directly who'd done this to her; what happened to her in the jail. But if she didn't talk, I was prepared to leave and let her continue on in rest.

That's when her lower lip started trembling. A tear escaped from the corner of her puffy eye.

"Honey, what's the matter?" My instinct was to reach out again, but I caught myself before crossing her no-touch boundary twice.

Slowly, and obviously painfully, she wiped the tear away with the back of her bruised hand. "Forget 'em."

"Forget who?"

"Family."

I couldn't very well tell her I seconded her motion 'cause I knew her words was coming from emotion and maybe even some medication.

"Chile, you *alive*! Don't worry about them. Right now, you

135

just concentrate on getting better. I been playin' the Bible CDs
to help you keep your mind stayed on the right path. I'mma
come back later on today and read you some books. I know
your body's fighting the battle, but it's gonna be the Word that
gives the fuel. You've come this far already by faith!"

She swallowed hard. "Did you sing that song to me?"

I giggled. "Sure did. And you sang it right back."

"Mmm. Thank you."

And with that, she slipped into sleep again.

Exiting her room, I stopped by the nurse's station to thank
them for their work. "You all doing a great job with her."

"Thank you," the one with the skinny frame and long
fingernails said. "It's our pleasure."

"Where's her guard? I wanted to thank him, too."

"Oh, she doesn't have one. She's free. The city dropped the
case, I guess."

"Don't say?"

"Yes, ma'am."

"So she can have visitors?"

"Yes, ma'am."

I notified Frank and he came right on in. We entered
Falanda's room and my husband prayed over her as she
continued to rest. "Lord, we thank You for Your healing
power, available to us through the blood of Christ. It's because
of Your loving kindness that our sister has been spared. We
pray now for continued healing, for full restoration so that
Your name may be glorified in all the earth. We pray also for
the person or persons who assaulted our sister. Soften their
hearts, Lord. Let them come to know you in the pardon of their
sin. Send laborers to speak life into them as well. In Jesus'
name, Amen."

"Amen."

Frank gave her a good once-over and nodded. "I believe she'll be just fine."

"I believe it, too."

Frank and I were stopped by several people as we strode through the hospital on our way out. His co-workers and friends wanted to know how things went at the conference. He told them all the same thing, "As good as can be expected without my wife there." He'd pat my hand, which was latched onto his bent arm.

Now, I know his answer came off as a joke since, technically, we still newlyweds. Hadn't been together five years yet. But I detected a little slice of truth in his words. I made myself a note to clear my schedule for Frank's conferences. *Maybe I could get myself something other than a coloring book next time.*

Since Frank had already planned to take off Monday to recover from jetlag, we sat up late that Sunday talking through the situation with Falanda. We both decided that, more than likely, the police decided it best to let the case drop to keep from any negative publicity. Wasn't worth whatever money and credibility it would cost them to bear the stain of suspicion.

"Whatever they can do to sweep this under the rug, they'll do," Frank said. "No city wants bad P-R; it brings out the press beehive, keeps visitors away, makes home values drop, lowers the tax base. Domino effect."

"Mmm hmm," I agreed. I loved to hear Frank talk politics. So smart.

"Have you given any thought to Falanda's rehab?"

"No. Not really."

"When they dismiss her, she may need some more recovery

time at home."

I really hadn't thought that far ahead. Of course, if I were single, living in my own home, there'd be no question. This woman was charged to my care by both Mt. Zion and the Lord Himself until she was well enough to leave.

Frank, however, might not consider himself part of the welcome wagon.

Shrugging, I asked, my eyes on the television as Frank flipped through channels, "What do you think?"

He focused on the tube, too. "You want her to stay with us, right?"

My hand flew to his arm. "Oh, Frank, it's not just her physical rehab, it's her mind. If she goes back to be nurtured by her family, she'll be beat-down all over again. After two days with them, I see why she's the way she is. Growing up in shame, guilt, ridicule. Honey, that's verbal abuse."

"But she's in her 40s at least," Frank countered.

"Don't matter. Sometimes, you just don't *know* until you see something different with your own eyes. You can watch TV and read books, but when you turn off the tube or close that book, you still got your own reality starin' back at you. And it speaks louder to some people. I...I can't send her back. Not until I pump some more Word and a whole lotta love into her. Those two together can change anybody from the inside out.

"Now, she don't have to stay with us. I'll use the rent money from the house, put her up in a hotel for a week or so. Can't be the Best Western, but anything's better than her going home in a weak state."

Frank smiled at me. "I'll leave it up to you and the Lord, B."

Chapter 19

Monday morning, I called Mr. Atkins and told him that Falanda's case had been dropped. He hinted that he'd gotten a call from the police department and heard them out without informing them that he was no longer Falanda's attorney—they didn't ask.

"Sounded to me as though they were getting a bit antsy about the video. The comments on that one website alone questioned the policemen's handling of the women."

Mr. Atkins seemed to agree with Frank about why they dropped the case.

"I need to go pick up her belongings. She'll be with me for a while after she's released. I was thinking they'd release her stuff to you, maybe, since I'm not family."

"We can try."

So Mr. Atkins and I went to get Falanda's personal belongings later that day. Thankfully, they did give her things to him in a large brown envelope.

He handed the package over to me in the outside hallway. "They're going to take care of her hospital bill as well," he told me with a smile. "It's probably more than she would have won in a case anyway."

"Oh, bless the Lord."

"Agreed." He held out his hand to shake. "Best to you, Mrs. Wilson."

"Just a second." I opened my wallet, then pressed three hundred-dollar bills into his hand. "I know a lawyer's time is valuable. You done put a lot of time and energy into this case—met with the police, been to the hospital, briefed us at the restaurant. And I'm pretty sure Falanda wouldn't be gettin' off so easy if you hadn't had a hand in it."

He nodded and tucked the money in his pocket. "Thank you so much."

"Same here."

That was the last I seen of Mr. Atkins.

Since Falanda's clothes had been sitting in an envelope in the back of who-knows-where for several days, I figured they could use a good washing. When I got home, I took the envelope straight to the laundry room. I opened the seal and slid the contents top of the dryer. Her purse, earrings, a pair of jeans, a pink top, tennis shoes with socks, and her big ole Donna Summer lookin' wig had been stuffed inside carelessly.

Something else caught my eye, though. Something small, shiny, and circular. I lifted the object out and realized—it was something of *mine!*

There in my hand, straight from Falanda's pocket, was a ring that my first husband gave me on my thirtieth birthday, which also happened to be the day I got baptized fully knowing what it meant. I twirled the gold band with three small diamond chips between my fingers, so small they were probably worth less than a hundred, yet priceless to me.

Somehow, I had to replay my actions over and over before it hit me: *Miss Falanda was intendin' to steal this ring from me.*

I high-tailed it to Frank's study. "Frank!"

He looked up from his Bible. "Yes?"

I walked toward him, holding the ring as though I'd just found something I'd never seen before. "Look at this."

Frank raised his chin so he could see through the bottom part of his bifocals. "What's that?"

"It's a ring. Albert gave it to me." Now that I'd said the words, the pang in my heart hit me strong.

Frank took the ring from me. Studied it for a second. "It's nice."

"Yeah, it's nice enough but I found it Falanda's pocket! I do believe she was going to take it from me."

"You mean *steal* it?"

"That's what I said!"

Frank shook his head and thrust the ring back into my hand. "B, she can't stay here when she's released."

"You ain't said nothin' but a word." I stamped my foot as angry tears escaped my eyes. "Ooh! I was trying so hard to help her," squeaked out of my mouth.

"I didn't say you couldn't help her. I'm just saying she can't stay here while you do," Frank clarified.

"But I don't *want* to help her. Not after *this*!"

Frank closed his Bible and walked me to the chaise. "B, sit down. Breathe."

Tears swam downstream from my eyes. "You know what? I'm tired of people using me."

"Wait, wait, wait. B. Shhh," Frank wiped my tears. "Baby. *People* aren't using you. *God's* using you."

"Using me to get my stuff stole?"

"No. Listen. It's not about the stuff. Everything we both have came from the Lord. The reason she can't stay here is because, obviously, valuable things are a temptation for her. The real issue is...she must have taken this from you before the fight. Correct?"

Still staring down at the ring now perched on my knee, I said, "Yes."

"So this is all stuff she did before the Word began to work in her heart, right?"

I had to agree.

"You said yourself that the Word of God, couched in love, can change a person from the inside out. Right?"

"Mmm hmm." My eyes stayed fixed on the ring while anger and the idea of mercy warred within me.

Frank cupped my chin and looked me in the eye. "She *can* change. Not saying she will, but if there's anything that has the power to change a person, it's His love and His word. I know because *He* changed *me*."

"He changed me, too," I admitted. *But I didn't steal nobody's ring.*

I protested softly, "It's just...I can put up with a lot of stuff. A fighter, a cusser, a drunk—but a thief. That's dirty to the core."

Frank grinned slightly. "A thief is just someone who doesn't think God is looking out for them. They need to meet El Roi, the God who sees. And B, I think you're the perfect person to make the introduction. Now, you started this thing with Falanda. Don't uproot what you've planted before it has a chance to take root."

I sniffed, taking in Frank's words, feeling that hum of truth in my spirit.

It was then that I got the revelation: The same thing I wanted Falanda and her family to do—forget her past and move forward in faith—was what I would have to do in order to carry on with the work of the Lord 'cause I, too, had come too far to turn around.

Chapter 20

The Lord's talk with me sounded a lot like Frank's. Both of 'em were right. My biggest problem was getting over myself so I wouldn't taint what God was doing with my feelings of being betrayed.

That was then. This is now.

I decided the best thing to do was be generous with Falanda. Let her know that she didn't have to take nothing from me because, more than likely, I was willing to give it to her if she just ask. Everything I got came from Him, anyway.

The only other person I told about the ring incident was Libby, and that was because I knew she had a special compassion for thieves—I'm sorry, ex-thieves. When one of her kin owed a bookie some money, they had some situations where some stuff came up missing in their house. Libby was embarrassed, but she told me about it. We prayed about it. Took some time and a few stints in rehab, but Libby's niece finally saw the light of Christ. Then we all had to forgive her and let go her past, just like now.

"B, I think what Frank said to you last night was absolutely divine. Tell you what. I've got a perfect solution."

"What you got up your sleeve, Libby?"

"You'll find out soon enough."

It was hard splitting my time between Frank, Jeffrey, churches, the exercise class, and Falanda over the next week, but the Lord graced me to do it all for the time being. Of course, Libby joined me when she could. Ophelia, too, once she got over the fact that the woman we was prayin' for had been kicked out the revival.

"B, why didn't you send an emergency breakthrough call to the ship?!" Ophelia fussed as we tidied up the church before Wednesday night service.

Good thing I didn't tell her about the ring.

"Wasn't nothin' you and Pastor could do out on the ocean!"

"I could have prayed!"

I picked up a fan off the floor. "You 'posed to be prayin' anyway. Without ceasing."

Ophelia busted out laughing at me. I joined her—I did tickle myself sometimes.

Me and Ophelia done prayed for a lot of rascals and done been together for plenty bedside conversions and recommitments. Ministering to Falanda, however, was a little harder than most. She had a lot of stuff she needed undone before she could accept the truth.

I mean, some people be like a clean slate. All you got to do is share the good news of Christ and they be glad to have it written on their heart. But people like Falanda—seem like you got to wipe off all the other nonsense and half-truths from their slates first. Then you can talk truth. Double-work for me and my friends, but we were up to the challenge.

That hospital room became Bible-study and prayer-central, honey. We might as well have brought in a chalkboard. Falanda might not have been to a seminary and learned all the

145

Greek and Hebrew words, but she was in the school of the Holy Ghost—He's the best teacher anyway!

"So, you're saying that God *wants* to forgive people," Falanda asked incredulously.

Ophelia and I nodded as I confirmed, "Yes! He's quick to forgive, the Bible says. Full of lovingkindness and tender mercy."

"Show me."

"Okay. Let's go to Psalm 103." Seemed like this was the theme chapter for Falanda.

Over and over again, she demanded: *Show me. Show me. Show me.* And every time, me and Ophelia backed it up with the holy Scriptures—Old and New Testament. Seeing the scriptures through her awe-struck eyes gave me even more of an appreciation for His heart toward us.

I noticed Falanda didn't take too well to Libby at first. Probably because she's white. But chile, Libby got to pointing to the scriptures and those scales of prejudice fell straight off Falanda's eyes when the truth came flowing out Libby's mouth.

Sometimes, Falanda would be stumped. "How could I have been this wrong all my life? How could I have told all those people how mad God was when, actually, He's not even in a bad mood?"

Libby, unaware of Falanda's no-touch rule, patted her on the shoulder. "You didn't know. But now you do."

To my surprise, Falanda didn't flinch. She didn't chastise Libby. She just let it all happen.

I guess about five days into our "University," I could tell Falanda was just about back to herself. We were sitting up watching an old episode of Andy Griffith, sort of taking a break until Ophelia was to come in another half hour or so.

I asked, "Honey, you feeling stronger?"

"Yes. I may be discharged tomorrow."

"Oh, good. Soon as they let you out, we'll get your strength up even more before you go back. I got another hotel in mind for you."

"No, Mama B, I couldn't ask you to—"

"You didn't ask. I offered." I smiled at my star pupil. As much as I hated she got beat up in the jail, look like that whole experience prepared her heart to figure out another way to live—and God just stepped right on in. Her whole demeanor was softer, less guarded. That's what happens to you when you know He loves you; you stop worryin' 'bout if you good enough, if somebody judgin' you, who might be out to hurt you. They can't touch you even if they do mean harm.

"Falanda, I been meaning to ask you. When your family came, they got an attorney for you. His name Mr. Atkins. He was thinkin' you might have a case against the police department, depending on what happened to you in there. Now, Sadie and Paul Jr. decided not to use his services after all, but if you think we should call him, let me know."

Falanda shook her head. "No. There's no case. No case we can prove anyway, though I'm pretty sure that wack officer put me in a cell with an even wackier Attila-the-Hun-looking chick on purpose. I only remember that she and I started arguing. And then I pushed her. That's the last thing I recall." Falanda placed her palm against her forehead. "I can't believe I don't remember. It's as though I completely blacked-out, even before I went unconscious."

I pulled her hand down, lowered it to the rail. "Don't even try. I been around a long time. I heard a lot of people say they blacked out during this-or-that. Let me tell you: Most the time, that black-out was a blessing from God. I don't care what them psychologists say, some stuff you don't *need* to remember. If your mind buries it, you might be better off not digging it up."

Falanda laughed, but stopped to wince and rub her jaw. "Ouchy, ouchy, ouchy."

"And speaking of stuff you don't need to revisit," I continued, "you might want to think about making some changes when you do go home to Cobble City."

"Changes like what?"

"For one thing, you got to keep learning the Word for yourself."

"Definitely," Falanda agreed.

"And you got to close yourself off to negativity," I suggested without naming names.

"What negativity?"

In my mind, I had rehearsed how to say the words, but now my invisible script was gone. *Help me, Lord.* "Anybody who constantly reminds you of what you can't do, what you can't have, who you'll never be…you gotta tune them out. Much as you love them and they might love you, you're not who other people say you are. You are who this Word says you are." I held up the Bible and gently tapped it on her forehead. "A new circle of friends would be helpful. I'm sure whatever church you find that preaches the Word will have a women's ministry. I want you to study up under somebody that's free in Christ."

"Yes, ma'am."

I nearly laughed at myself. *I'm starting to sound like Frank.*

Her last morning in the hospital, Falanda was sitting on her bed, obviously waiting for me. She had tears in her eyes, and her hands were wringing something awful.

"What is it, baby? This is a joyous occasion! You're about to be dismissed!" I said, walking toward her.

"Mama B, there's something I need to tell you."

I stood over her, stroking her shoulder gently. "Whatever is it?"

She looked up at me. The tears gave way. "I took something from you. A ring. I was…it was in a drawer. And I was jealous because you had a nice house, and you were so open and loving…I…thought you were so naïve. I wanted you to be as guarded and paranoid about people as me, I guess. So I took the ring. To hurt you, like *I* was hurting. I'm so sorry."

She fell into my side and I hugged her. "I forgive you, Falanda." *Thank You, Lord, for letting me see this through until the end. I love how You work.*

"Now I want to tell you something," I confessed. "I knew about the ring."

Shock streaked across her face. "You did?"

"Mmm hmmm. Found it in your pocket when I started washing the clothes they was holdin' at the police station."

Her mouth was still open. I closed it by pushing her chin up gently.

"That ring meant a lot to me because I got it on my birthday, which was also the day I was baptized. In a way, the day you surrender to Him is a lot like your birthday—brand new life."

"Wow," she marveled. "I never thought of it like that. I mean, I still think it's terrible that I took the ring, though."

I pushed her up by the shoulders and eyed her. "Anything

else you took I need to know about?"

She laughed slightly, "No, ma'am."

"All right then." I rolled my eyes halfway. "Look. Let's forget about what you did before. Sometimes, we need to be real good forgetters. God's a master-forgetter, He put stuff far as the east is from the west! No reason why we can't aim to follow in His ways, you hear?"

She attempted to smile.

"So now, let's make today *your* birthday." I took the wrapped box from my purse that sweet Libby had given me to pass on to Falanda.

"For me?"

"Yes siree."

Tearfully, Falanda opened it and found a ring of her own, just as dainty and simple as mine. "Wait—you're *giving* me a ring?"

"Yep. Every time you wear it, I want you think about how God used this period in your life to make you all over again. This is *your* birthday time."

Falanda slid the ring on her pinky finger. She pulled me into the biggest hug and just let the tears rip. She wailed, "Nobody's ever treated me like this before. Never. *Ever.*"

"It's called the love of Christ, honey. That's exactly what it is."

You real good, God. Real good.

Chapter 21

Even funnier than me sounding like Frank was what happened when Falanda got out of the hospital. I got her a room at that new Holiday Inn Express. It was out the way, so I had to get over there early to check on her—wouldn't be no late-night visits.

Anyhow, her right hand was kind of sprained. I'm not sure exactly how somebody's hand gets sprained, but I suppose in a fight, anything's possible.

She had to stretch it ever so often, keep the fine muscles moving.

You know what we ended up doing together? Coloring in that book! *Ha!* I tell you, we loved it. We'd sit there and color for hours, just talking. She'd ask something about Jesus and I'd tell her, of course, but we were up to the personal connecting part now. Every time she told me a story about something that happened in her childhood, I'd comment in a way that showed her how God loved her. Ain't no way of knowing what all foolishness been spoken into somebody's, life but I know one thing: When the truth shows up, lies ain't got a leg to stand on.

Over crayons and coloring patterns, she confided, "My mother used to tell me all the time that she wished I was never born. She said she was so busy partying and living it up in the clubs, she didn't realize she was pregnant until it was too late to have an abortion at her clinic; that's the only reason I'm here."

My heart could have ripped open right there—who tells their kid something like that? Then I remembered the last young lady the Lord sent my way. Danielle, whose real name was actually "Trouble." Her Momma had a problem, too. Look like the Lord wanted me to do a lot of mothering on these younger ladies.

Anyhow, the coloring provided a quiet, safe, calm mood. I didn't look up from that hibiscus flower. "Well, that ain't the whole truth. I mean, maybe your Momma didn't know she was pregnant, and maybe she didn't plan for you, but God did. Ever think maybe He's the one who hid you inside of her until she couldn't do nothing about it?"

Falanda chuckled. "Never thought of it like that."

Even for some of the real bad stuff, I'd say, "You know that wasn't your fault, right?"

And somehow, because someone twenty years older was saying it, look like the burdens were rolling away one-by-one. It came as a total shock to her that God wasn't holding her accountable for her mother or her father, and she didn't have to be like them. She could be more and more like Christ every day.

"Finished!" she announced, massaging her hands.

I looked over at her work: A mighty fine coloring of blue sky over a waterfall and trees at some place called Shawnee National Forest in Illinois. "Why Falanda, you are quite the artist, I see."

"You like it?"

Her grin reminded me of my own children, looking for approval and acceptance.

"It's beautiful."

"I want you to have it," she said. "You've given me so much. Please. Let me give you something from my heart, Mama B."

I held the paper in the air, studied its soothing colors again. "I receive it gladly."

And just like that, the full circle of His love had come right back to me.

Epilogue

Me and Falanda kept in touch real close right after she left. Seemed like every night, she called me crying 'bout something her Aunt Sadie had said. Now that she'd opened her heart to the love of the Lord, she was trying to be her new sweet self, but Sadie didn't want the new Falanda. She wanted the fightin' Falanda.

So I told Falanda point-blank, "Honey, you gon' have to stop working at your aunt's shop and get another job that pays more so you can move out on your own."

"Move out?"

"Yes. Move out."

She hesitated. "But...my Momma grew up here. My aunt lives here, my brother is here. This was my grandmother's house."

"Honey, look at the scriptures and look at your ring. Just 'cause that's what they all did don't mean it's what you have to do. If you comin' under constant attack there, you got to make a move. I'd tell you the same thing if you was with an abusive man!"

She snarked, "You wouldn't have to tell me that—I wouldn't take it!"

"Same thing," I connected the dots for her.

Honey, next thing I knew, Falanda had got herself a job somewhere in Grand Prairie, which is about an hour west of me and an hour and a half east of her folks, if you drivin' real fast. She said she couldn't find a good church right away, so she was going to start coming to Mt. Zion every Sunday for now.

Oh, it was such a joy to see her again! Her face back to normal size, her body moving without a limp. Even more important, she was radiant with the love of Christ. Told she couldn't go back to her old church or stay around her people too long 'cause once she got a taste of freedom in Him, it's just too hard to go back and live under all that condemnation, guilt, and bondage.

Pretty soon, her new persona and gentler ways caught Rev. Martin's eye. Honey, she didn't just catch it, she put it in a jar and locked it up. Them two started going to dinners with Pastor and Ophelia. Then the two couples came over to our house for Christmas breakfast.

By that following Valentine's Day, Rev. Martin and Falanda were engaged to be married. I'd never seen either of them so happy! They was already bringing some kind of couple's conference to Peasner, talking about how to pray together when you both have busy schedules—something or another like that.

And to think, I almost missed out on seeing the goodness of the Lord over my hurt feelings! If it hadn't of been for Frank, I probably would have.

I do believe he deserves a sweet potato pie.

Discussion Questions

1. The first night of the revival, Falanda refused to pray for a new television for Henrietta because Henrietta said she wanted to watch a reality show with the blessing. Do you think the minister was wrong in her refusal? Have you ever prayed for something that, in retrospect, turned out to be detrimental?

2. How would you describe Falanda's attitude with the police officer at the hotel? Was she justifiably angry? What about the officer—was he wrong? Was Mama B right or wrong in telling Falanda that she should have respected the officer's authority?

3. Mama B says she was tired, sleepy, and out way too late, which caused her to be snappy with Falanda after the first night of the revival. How does physical stress affect your emotions?

4. Though Mama B disagrees with Falanda's theology, she does give Falanda credit for moving forward in faith with what she believes the Lord has called her to do. Do you think God honors it when people start where they are with what they know—or is it important to wait until you know more before getting started? How does one know when they know "enough"?

5. When Mama B first discovers the video, she's humiliated. Yet the person who posted it and those who have watched and made comments obviously think it's funny. Have you ever stopped to consider if the videos you find funny on social media would be as funny if you were in the subject's shoes?

6. Frank doesn't want Mama B to spend too much money to

help Falanda get out of jail. How far are you willing to go to help someone who really doesn't deserve help? How far did Christ go for us? How do you know the difference between helping someone and enabling them?

7. Mama B has some poignant thoughts about why the African-American community handled its business without involvement from police, right or wrong. How have your experiences shaped your views of law enforcement? Have recent events in the media changed your view?

8. When Falanda's family comes to town, Mama B has a bit of a grudge against them and even lets them spend the night in their car. Do you find it hard to deal with people who appear to have ill motives? Should she have let them stay at her house?

9. Paul Jr. thought that Al Sharpton was going to come to Peasner, but Mama B told him she didn't think that would be the case since the officer wasn't white. Do you agree or disagree with Mama B? How do you separate human rights issues from race issues? Are they always one and the same?

10. Mama B came to the realization that Falanda was her assignment—not Falanda's family. Was she right to stop dealing with them? How do you deal with negative family members?

11. When Sadie tells Mama B about Falanda's family tree, Mama B tells her that the blood of Christ is what matters above all. Who do you consider your *real* family—those who are born of natural relation or those who are born again with you in faith? Is there a difference?

12. Frank tells Mama B that she's never more like Christ than when she sacrificially loves someone who doesn't deserve it. Have you had an experience where you loved someone

in spite of how they were acting?

13. Mama B advises Falanda to meet some new friends, maybe visit another church, so that she won't fall under the negative influence of Aunt Sadie. She had to walk a fine line between speaking the truth and insulting Falanda's family. How would you have handled it?

A Note from the Author

Though Mama B is a fictional character, the God she serves is not. If you have yet to start your journey in Christ, let me encourage you to seek Him. Seek Him in all of his glory, all of His love, and His wisdom. If you feel the tug in your heart, Thank Him for His goodness, ask Him for forgiveness, and invite His Son, Jesus Christ to live in you. He stands knocking on the door of your heart and is more than pleased to pay for your sin. It's a hard, cold life without Him. I pray that the warmth of His love will be your constant companion.

Other Books by Michelle Stimpson

Christian Fiction

A Forgotten Love (Novella) Book One in the "A Few Good Men" Series

The Start of a Good Thing (Novella) Book Two in the "A Few Good Men" Series

A Shoulda Woulda Christmas (Novella)

Boaz Brown (Book 1 in the Boaz Brown Series)

No Weapon Formed (Book 2 in the Boaz Brown Series)

Divas of Damascus Road

Falling into Grace

I Met Him in the Ladies' Room (Novella)

I Met Him in the Ladies' Room Again (Novella)

Last Temptation (Starring "Peaches" from *Boaz Brown*)

Mama B: A Time to Speak (Book 1)

Mama B: A Time to Dance (Book 2)

Mama B: A Time to Love (Book 3)

Mama B: A Time to Mend (Book 4)

Mama B: A Time for War (Book 5)

Someone to Watch Over Me

Stepping Down

The Good Stuff

The Blended Blessings Series (co-authored with CaSandra McLaughlin)

Trouble In My Way (Young Adult)

What About Momma's House? (Novella with April Barker)

What About Love? (Novella with April Barker)

What About Tomorrow? (Novella with April Barker)

Non-Fiction

Did I Marry the Wrong Guy? And other silent ponderings of a fairly normal Christian wife

Uncommon Sense: 30 Truths to Radically Renew Your Mind in Christ

The 21-Day Publishing Plan

If you like Michelle Stimpson's books, you'll want to meet her literary friends!
BlackChristianReads.com

About the Author

Michelle Stimpson's works include the highly acclaimed *Boaz Brown, Divas of Damascus Road* (National Bestseller), and *Falling Into Grace,* which has been optioned for a movie of the week. She has published several short stories for high school students through her educational publishing company at WeGottaRead.com.

Michelle serves in women's ministry at her home church, Oak Cliff Bible Fellowship. She regularly speaks at special events and writing workshops sponsored churches, schools, book clubs, and educational organizations.

The Stimpsons are proud parents of two young adults—one in the military, one in college—and a weird Cocker Spaniel named MiMi.

Visit Michelle online:
www.MichelleStimpson.com
www.Facebook.com/michelle.stimpson2

Made in the USA
Middletown, DE
21 April 2018